Ben Jonson's The Arraignment, or Poetaster: A Retelling

David Bruce

Published by David Bruce, 2022.

This is a work of fiction. Similarities to real people, places, or events are entirely coincidental.

BEN JONSON'S THE ARRAIGNMENT, OR POETASTER: A RETELLING

First edition. July 10, 2022.

Copyright © 2022 David Bruce.

ISBN: 979-8201400576

Written by David Bruce.

Table of Contents

Educate Yourself
Read Like A Wolf Eats
Be Excellent to Each Other
Books Then, Books Now, Books Forever

In this retelling, as in all my retellings, I have tried to make the work of literature accessible to modern readers who may lack the knowledge about mythology, religion, and history that the literary work's contemporary audience had.

Do you know a language other than English? If you do, I give you permission to translate this book, copyright your translation, publish or self-publish it, and keep all the royalties for yourself. (Do give me credit, of course, for the original retelling.)

I would like to see my retellings of classic literature used in schools, so I give permission to the country of Finland (and all other countries) to give copies of any or all of my retellings to all students forever. I also give permission to the state of Texas (and all other states) to give copies of any or all of my retellings to all students forever. I also give permission to all teachers to give copies of any or all of my retellings to all students forever. Of course, libraries are welcome to use my eBooks for free.

Teachers need not actually teach my retellings. Teachers are welcome to give students copies of my eBooks as background material. For example, if they are teaching Homer's *Iliad* and *Odyssey*, teachers are welcome to give students copies of my *Virgil's* Aeneid: *A Retelling in Prose* and tell them, "Here's another ancient epic you may want to read in your spare time."

CAST OF CHARACTERS

Male Characters

AUGUSTUS CAESAR. *Emperor of Rome.*

MAECENAS. *Poet and patron; counselor to Augustus Caesar.*

MARCUS OVID. *Father to PUBLIUS OVID.*

LUSCUS. *Servant to MARCUS and PUBLIUS OVID.*

TIBULLUS. *Elegiac poet.*

CORNELIUS GALLUS *Elegiac poet.*

PROPERTIUS. *Elegiac poet. Sextus Propertius.*

FUSCUS ARISTIUS. *Scholar and writer, friend of HORACE.*

PUBLIUS OVID. *Publius Ovidius Naso, elegiac poet. Referred to mostly as OVID in this book, and sometimes as young Ovid or Ovid the poet or Publius Ovid. His father will always be OVID SENIOR. Ovid wrote* Ars Amatoria [The Art of Love] *and* Metamorphoses.

VIRGIL. *Publius Virgilius Maro, epic poet, author of* Aeneid.

HORACE. *Quintus Horatius Flaccus, satirical poet, author of* Satires.

TREBATIUS. *Lawyer, friend of HORACE.*

LUPUS. *Tribune. Asinius Lupus.*

TUCCA. *Military man, sort of. He has a stutter and/or sputters at times, as when his emotions are strong or when he is pretending that his emotions are strong. Pantilius Tucca.*

CRISPINUS. *The Poetaster. Poetasters are poets who write bad poetry. Rufus Laberius Crispinus.*

HERMOGENES. *Musician and singer.*

DEMETRIUS FANNIUS. *Hack writer.*

ALBIUS. *Tradesman, husband to CHLOE.*

MINOS. *Apothecary, aka pharmacist.*

HISTRIO. *Actor.*

AESOP. *Actor.*

PYRGI. *Pages to TUCCA. The singular is Pyrgus.*

LICTORS.

EQUITES ROMANI. *Knights. Members of the Equestrian class.*

Female Characters

JULIA. *Daughter to AUGUSTUS CAESAR.*

CYTHERIS. *PROPERTIUS' love.*
PLAUTIA. *TIBULLUS' love.*
CHLOE. *Wife to ALBIUS.*
MAIDS.
In the Induction
ENVY.
PROLOGUE. *(Heroic Virtue). The Prologue speaks the prologue at or near the beginning of the play.*
THE SCENE: ROME
NOTES:

An arraignment is a calling to account, such as calling an accused person into a courtroom to defend him- or herself. Or it can mean a denunciation.

In Ben Jonson's society, a person of higher rank would use "thou," "thee," "thine," and "thy" when referring to a person of lower rank. (These terms were also used affectionately and between equals.) A person of lower rank would use "you" and "your" when referring to a person of higher rank.

"Sirrah" was a title used to address someone of a social rank inferior to the speaker. Friends, however, could use it to refer to each other.

The word "wench" in Ben Jonson's time was not necessarily negative. It was often used affectionately.

The poetaster, Crispinus, is a parody of the playwright John Marston, with whom Ben Jonson had a feud. The two men were sometimes frienemies.

Ben Jonson's play conflates Julia the Elder (Augustus Caesar's daughter), and Julie the Younger (Augustus Caesar's granddaughter, the daughter of Julia the Elder).

Roman Offices
Consuls: The office of Consul was the highest political office of the Roman Republic. Two Consuls were elected each year and served for one year.

Praetors: A Praetor can be 1) the commander of an army, or 2) a magistrate. The office of Praetor (magistrate) was the second highest political office of the Roman Republic. They were subject only to the veto of the Consuls. Praetors could take the auspices, the performance of which was a religious rite. Taking the auspices was a way of (supposedly) foretelling the future.

Lictors: Lictors served the Consuls and carried rods and axes as symbols of the Senators' authority. Rods were symbols of the Consuls' power to inflict corporal punishment, and axes were symbols of their power to inflict capital punishment. Lictors executed punishments on people who had been convicted of serious crimes.

Tribunes: Tribunes were administrative officers. Some were judicial Tribunes, and some were military Tribunes.

Aediles: An Aedile was a Roman magistrate who was in charge of maintaining public buildings. They also organized public festivals and were in charge of weights and measures.

Censors: They supervised public morality and maintained the census.

Prefects: They had civil or military power, but that power was delegated to them from others.

Praecones: Heralds. Criers in meetings of the Senate. They cried loudly things during a trial, such as "Silence!"

THE INDUCTION

The induction — introduction — of this play began with the second sounding of a trumpet. The first sounding was a warning for the audience to begin taking their seats. The third sounding would be a notice that the play was starting. Envy arrived at the second sounding in order to speak before the real Prologue arrived.

Like other denizens of hell in plays, Envy arose from a trapdoor in the stage floor. Several snakes were entwined around her arms and hung from her neck.

Envy said to herself, "Light, I salute thee, but with wounded nerves, wishing that thy golden splendor were pitchy darkness."

Some plays at this time had the title of the play written on a title board on stage.

Envy looked at the title board and said, "What's here? *The Arraignment?* Aye: this, this is it that our sunken eyes have stayed awake and waited for all this while. Here will be the subject matter for my snakes and me.

"Cling to my neck and wrists, my loving worms — my loving snakes — and cast yourselves round in soft and amorous folds until I bid thee to uncurl. Then break your knots and shoot out yourselves at length, as if your forced stings would hide themselves within the regarded-with-malice sides of him to whom I shall apply you."

Envy was hostile to Ben Jonson, the playwright. She wanted her snakes of envy to bite his sides, which she hated, and she would force them to do that.

Envy looked at the audience and the stage candles and said, "Wait! The shine of this assembly here offends my sight. I'll darken that first and outface — confront and disconcert — their grace."

Envy blew out some candles that provided light for the stage.

She then said to the audience:

"Don't marvel if I stare and glare at you. These past fifteen weeks — as long as it took Ben Jonson to turn the embryo of the plot into a finished play — have I with burning lights — my eyes — mixed vigilant thoughts in expectation of this hated play, which will criticize envious slanderers. But now at last I have arrived as its Prologue.

"Nor would I desire that you should look for other looks, gestures, or expressions of compliment and courtesy from me than what the infected bulk — breast — of Envy can furnish.

"For I have arisen here with a covetous hope to blast your pleasures and destroy your sports with wrong-headed wrestings of meanings, wrong-headed comments and explanations, wrong-headed applications of supposed allusions to real people and real events, spy-like suggestions, private whisperings, and a thousand such promoting sleights and sly tricks as these.

Envy was planning on traducing the play with her lies and false interpretations.

She said, "Closely notice how I will begin: the scene is —"

She then looked at the location signs on stage.

Envy said, "Ha! 'Rome'? 'Rome'? And 'Rome'?"

She then said to herself:

"Crack, eye-strings, and let your eyeballs drop onto the earth! Let me be forever blind!

"I am forestalled; all my hopes are crossed, checked, and abated. Bah, a freezing sweat flows forth at all my pores; my entrails burn!

"What should I do? 'Rome'? 'Rome'?

"O my vexed soul, how might I force an application of this play to the present state?"

In other words: If this play is set in Rome, how could it apply to England and its government and society?

Obviously, it could apply to England and its government and society and to many other countries and their governments and societies. And it could apply to many different times, not just the present time. Satire is like that.

Obviously, Ben Jonson knew that, but he was afraid of being sued for libel.

If you want to satirize an Englishman, the safe thing to do is to pretend that the Englishman is a Roman.

Envy peered into the audience and said:

"Are there no actors here? No poet-apes — poor poets who try to imitate real poets — who come with basilisks' eyes, whose forked tongues are steeped in venom, as their hearts are steeped in gall?"

A basilisk was a mythological monster that could kill with a glance.

Envy continued:

"Either of these would help me; they could wrest, pervert, and poison all they hear or see with senseless glosses, interpretations, explanatory notes, and allusions."

Envy began to address the "good" devils she hoped were in the audience:

"Now, if you are good devils, don't flee from me.

"You know what dear, precious, and ample faculties I have endowed you good devils with; I'll lend you more.

"Here, take my snakes among you, come, and eat, and while the squeezed juice flows in your black jaws, help me to damn the author."

Black jaws are those that spew forth slander and malicious envy.

In art, Envy was often depicted as eating a snake.

Envy continued:

"Spit the juice forth upon his lines, and show your rusty — discolored and rotten — teeth at every word or accent.

"Or else each of you choose one of my longest vipers, to stick down in your deep throats, and let the heads come forth at your rank — gross and stinky — mouths so that he may see you armed with triple malice, to hiss, sting, and tear his work and him.

"The snake heads and their forked tongues may forge lies, and then declaim, traduce, corrupt, apply, spy and inform the authorities, suggest —

"Oh, these are gifts wherein your souls are blest."

No "good devils" spoke up. No one was willing to defame Ben Jonson.

Envy said:

"What! Do you hide yourselves? Will none appear? None answer? What! Does his calm troop of audience members frighten you?

"Nay, then I do despair."

She said to herself:

"Down, sink again. This travail is all lost with my dead hopes."

Envy had traveled and labored — travailed — to say the prologue.

She continued:

"If in such bosoms spite have left to dwell,

"Envy is not on earth, nor scarcely in hell."

Envy partially descended back into hell.

The trumpet sounded for the third time and the real Prologue, who was wearing armor, appeared on stage.

The Prologue said to Envy:

"Wait, monster, before thou sink beneath the stage."

The Prologue placed a foot on Envy's head and said:

"Thus on thy head we set our bolder, stronger foot, with which we tread thy malice into earth."

As Envy descended into hell, the Prologue said, "So spite should die, despised and scorned by noble industry such as the industry spent in writing this play."

Envy disappeared, and the Prologue said:

"If anyone should muse why I greet the stage in the guise of an armed Prologue, know that it is a dangerous age, wherein who writes had better present his scenes forty-fold proof against the conjuring, secretly-working-together means of base detractors and illiterate apes that fill up theater seats in fair and well-formed shapes.

"Against these we have put on this defense we are forced to wear, whereof the allegory and hidden sense is that a well-erected confidence can frighten their pride and laugh their folly away from here.

"Here now, suppose that our author should once more swear that his play were good — he implores you to not accuse him of arrogance, however much that common spawn of ignorance, our small-fry writers, may slime his fame and give his action that adulterated, corrupt name and title of arrogance.

"Such full-blown vanity he loathes more than base dejection; there's a mean between both. With a constant firmness he pursues that mean, as one who knows the strength of his own muse. And this he hopes all free souls will allow.

"Others, who take with a rugged brow and frown of displeasure his assertion that this play is good,

"Their moods he rather pities than maliciously envies.

"His mind is above their injuries."

CHAPTER 1

— 1.1 —

Publius Ovid read out loud from the new poem he was working on:

"*Then, when this body falls in funeral fire,*

"*My name shall live, and my best part aspire.*"

He then said, "It shall go so: My poem will end with these lines."

Luscus, his servant and the servant of Ovid's father, Marcus Ovid, aka Ovid Senior, entered the room and said, "Young master, Master Ovid, do you hear me? God save me! Away with your songs and sonnets and on with your gown and cap, quickly — here, here —"

He handed Ovid the garments.

Law students in Ben Jonson's England wore distinctive caps and gowns.

Luscus continued, "Your father will be a man of this room quickly. Come — nay, nay, nay, nay, be quick."

He took Ovid's poem from him and said, "These verses, too, a poison on them, I cannot abide them, they make me ready to vomit, by the banks of Helicon. Look what a rascally untoward — improper and foolish — thing this poetry is; I could tear them — your poems — now."

Helicon was a mountain sacred to the Muses. Its springs were also sometimes called Helicon.

As he took back his poem, Ovid said, "Give it to me."

He then asked, "How near is my father?"

Luscus answered, "By the heart of man! Get a law book in your hand; I will not answer you otherwise."

Ovid picked up a law book.

Luscus continued, "Why, good; now there's some formality in you. By Jove and three or four of the gods more, I am right of my old master's humor and opinion about that — we have the same opinion about your poems: This villainous poetry will undo you, by the welkin, aka heavens."

"What! Have thou buskins on, Luscus, that thou swear so tragically and high?" Ovid asked.

Buskins are thick-soled boots worn by actors in tragedies to give them added height and gravitas.

Luscus replied, "No, but I have boots on and I am prepared and ready for anything, sir, and your father also has boots on, too, by this time, for he called for them before I came from the lodging where he is staying in the city."

"Why, was he no more dressed than that?" Ovid asked.

Luscus said, "Oh, no; and there was the mad skeldering — begging — captain with the velvet arms — weapons carried in velvet scabbards — ready to lay hold on him as he comes down from his room — he who presses every man he meets, with an oath, to lend him money, and cries, 'Thou must do it, old boy, as thou are a man, a man of worship and worthiness.'"

"Who, Pantilius Tucca?" Ovid asked.

"Aye, he," Luscus answered, "and I met little Master Lupus, the Tribune, going thither, too."

Ovid said, "If my father is under their arrest — if Tucca and Lupus are detaining him — I may with safety enough read over my elegy before he comes here."

He put down the law book and picked up his poem.

"God save me!" Luscus said. "What'll you do? Why, young master, you are not Castalian-mad, lunatic, frantic, desperate? Huh? Are you?"

A Castalian-mad man is a poet made mad by poetic inspiration. The nymph Castalia turned herself into a spring at Delphi to escape the god Apollo. People who drank its waters became poetically inspired.

"What ails thou, Luscus?" Ovid said. "What is wrong with you?"

"God be with you, sir, and goodbye," Luscus said. "I'll leave you to your poetical fancies and furies. I'll not be guilty of encouraging you in such pursuits, I."

Luscus exited.

"Don't be guilty of that, good Ignorance," Ovid said.

"Good Ignorance" referred to Luscus.

Ovid continued:

"I'm glad thou are gone, for thus alone, our ear shall better judge the hasty errors of our morning muse."

He began to read his new poem out loud:

"Envy, why twitt'st thou me [by saying] my time's spent ill

"And call'st my verse fruits of an idle quill?
"Or that, unlike the [family] line from whence I sprung,
"War's dusty honors I pursue not young?
"Or that I study not the tedious laws
"And prostitute my voice in every cause?
"Thy scope is mortal, mine [is] immortal, fame,
"Which through the world shall ever chant my name.
"Homer will live whilst Tenedos stands, and Ide [Ida],
"Or to the sea fleet Simois doth [does] slide;"

Ovid wished to pursue immortal fame as a poet rather than be a soldier or a lawyer. Homer and other poets had achieved immortal fame for their poetry.

Homer is the author of the *Iliad* and the *Odyssey*. These works will last as long as Tenedos (an island), Ida (a mountain), and the Simois (a river), all of which are mentioned in Homer's epic poems, last.

To end the Trojan War, Odysseus came up with the idea of the Trojan Horse. The Trojan War had been fought for 10 years, and the forces of Agamemnon and the other Greeks had not been able to conquer Troy by might, and so Odysseus had the idea of using trickery to conquer Troy. The Greeks built a huge wooden horse and left it outside Troy, and then they seemed to sail away in their ships and return home. However, the Trojan Horse was hollow and filled with Greek soldiers, including Odysseus, and the ships sailed behind an island called Tenedos so that the Trojans could not see them. A lying Greek named Sinon stayed behind and pretended that he had escaped from Odysseus, who had wanted to kill him. Sinon told the Trojans that if they were to take the Trojan Horse inside the walls of Troy, then Troy would never fall. Amid great rejoicing, the Trojans took the Trojan Horse inside the walls of Troy. That night, the Greek warriors came out of the Trojan Horse, went to the gates of Troy, killed the Trojan guards, and opened the gates of Troy. Agamemnon and his troops were outside the gates, after returning from hiding behind the island. The Greeks then conquered Troy.

Ovid continued to read his poem out loud:

"And so shall Hesiod, too, while vines do bear
"Or crooked sickles crop the ripened ear."

Hesiod is the author of *Works and Days*, which praises labor and describes the five ages of Humankind, with the Age of Gold being the best.

Ovid continued to read his poem out loud:

"Callimachus, though in invention low,

"Shall still be sung, since he in art doth [does] flow."

Callimachus is a Greek poet whom some critics such as Ben Jonson thought was skillful but not inspired.

Ovid continued to read his poem out loud:

"No loss shall come to Sophocles' proud vein;"

Sophocles is the great Greek tragedian who wrote *Oedipus the King*, aka *Oedipus Rex*. In this tragedy, the Sphinx asks Oedipus this riddle: What goes on four legs in the morning, two legs at noon, and three legs in the evening? If Oedipus cannot answer this riddle correctly, the Sphinx will kill him. Fortunately, Oedipus does answer the riddle correctly: Man, who goes on hands and knees as a crawling baby, two legs as a healthy adult, and two legs and a cane as an old person.

Ovid continued to read his poem out loud:

"With sun and moon, Aratus shall remain."

Aratus is a Greek poet who wrote about the constellations.

Ovid continued to read his poem out loud:

"Whilst slaves be false, fathers hard, and bawds be whorish,

"Whilst harlots flatter shall Menander flourish."

Menander is a Greek comic playwright who wrote *Dyskolos*, aka *The Misanthrope*.

Ovid continued to read his poem out loud:

"Ennius, though rude [uneducated], and Accius' high-reared strain

"A fresh applause in every age shall gain."

Ennius, who used Greek literary models, is considered by some critics the father of Roman poetry.

Accius was a Roman tragedian who made free translations of plays by Greek tragedians, especially Aeschylus, who wrote the *Oresteia*, a trilogy of three tragedies: *Agamemnon*, *The Libation Bearers*, and *The Eumenides*. In the trilogy, Agamemnon returns home after he and the Greeks defeat Troy. His wife, Clytemnestra, who has taken a lover, murders him, and in turn, is murdered by their son, Orestes. The avenging spirits known as the Furies pursue him until finally the goddess Athena arranges a new function for them, transforming them into the Eumenides, aka the Kindly Ones.

Ovid continued to read his poem out loud:

"*Of Varro's name what ear shall not be told?*

"*Of Jason's Argo, and the fleece of gold?*"

The Roman writer Varro wrote about the Latin language.

Jason and his Argonauts built a ship named the *Argo* and sailed to Colchis to get the Golden Fleece. With the help of the witch Medea, they got the Golden Fleece and sailed home with it.

Ovid continued to read his poem out loud:

"*Then shall Lucretius' lofty numbers [verses] die*

"*When earth and seas in fire and flames shall fry.*"

The Roman Lucretius wrote a book of philosophy titled *De Rerum Natura*, aka *Concerning the Nature of Things*.

Ovid continued to read his poem out loud:

"*Tityrus, Tillage, Aenee [Aeneid] shall be read*

"*Whilst Rome of all the conquered world is head.*"

These were three major works by Virgil. Tityrus is a narrator in Virgil's *Eclogues*, aka *Bucolics*, about pastoral life. The *Georgics* is about farming, or tillage. The *Aeneid* is Virgil's masterpiece. It tells the story of the Fall of Troy and how the Trojan prince Aeneas journeyed to Italy by way of Carthage to become an important ancestor of the Romans.

Ovid continued to read his poem out loud:

"*Till Cupid's fires be out and his bow broken*

"*Thy verses, neat [elegant] Tibullus, shall be spoken.*

"*Our Gallus shall be known from east to west;*

"*So shall Lycoris, whom he now loves best.*"

Tibullus and Gallus were two of Ovid's poet friends. Lycoris was the name Gallus gave to his lover in his poems.

Ovid continued to read out loud:

"*The suffering plowshare or the flint may wear,*

"*But heavenly poesy [poetry] no death can fear.*

"*Kings shall give place to it, and kingly shows,*

"*The banks over which gold-bearing Tagus flows.*"

The Tagus River divides Spain and Portugal.

Ovid continued to read his poem out loud:

"*Kneel hinds [Boors kneel] to trash; me let bright Phoebus swell*

"*With cups full flowing from the Muses' well.*"

In other words: "Boors kneel to trash; let bright Phoebus Apollo, god of poetry, fill me with inspiration."

Ovid continued to read his poem out loud:

"*Frost-fearing myrtle [an evergreen shrub that symbolizes immortality] shall impale [encircle] my head,*

"*And by sad lovers I'll be often read.*

"*Envy the living, not the dead, doth [does] bite,*"

In other words: Envy bites the living, not the dead.

Ovid continued to read out loud:

"*For after death all men receive their right.*

"*Then, when this body falls in funeral fire,*

"*My name shall live, and my best part aspire.*"

As an evergreen, myrtle does not fear literal frost; however, it does fear frost-brained poetasters who cannot write good poetry.

Ovid Senior, Luscus, Tucca, and Lupus entered the room.

Tucca was a military man, sort of. He was also a conman, definitely. Lupus was an official: a Tribune.

Ovid Senior, Ovid's father, who had heard the end of his son's poem, said:

"Your name shall live indeed, sir; you say true; but you don't think about how infamously, how scorned and contemned in the eyes and ears of the best and gravest Romans; you never so much as dream about that.

"Are these the fruits of all my travail and expenses? Is this the scope and aim of thy studies? Are these the hopeful courses wherewith I have so long flattered my expectation from thee?

"Verses? Poetry? Ovid, whom I thought to see the pleader in cases of law, has become Ovid the play-maker?"

"No, sir," Ovid, his son, said.

Ovid Senior said:

"Yes, sir. I hear that a tragedy of yours is coming forth for the common actors there, called *Medea*.

"By my household gods, I swear that if I come to the acting of it, I'll add one tragic part more than is yet expected to it; believe me when I promise it."

The Roman household gods are the Lares and the Penates, the ancestral gods and the gods of the pantry. When Aeneas fled from fallen Troy, he carried his father on his back, and his father held the household gods.

Ovid Senior continued, "What! Shall I have my son a stager now? An ingle for actors? A gull? A rook? A shot-clog?"

A "stager" is a contemptuous term for a theater-man.

An "ingle" is a young boy who is used for homosexual sex, but the term can also refer to a friend.

Gulls and rooks are fools.

A shot-clog is a fool who is tolerated because he pays the bills.

Ovid Senior continued, "To make suppers and be laughed at? Publius, I will set thee on the funeral pile first."

Publius Ovid, his son, said, "Sir, I beg you to have patience."

Luscus said to Ovid:

"Nay, this it is to have your ears dammed up to good counsel."

Luscus then said to the others:

"I did augur — predict — all this to him beforehand, without poring into an ox's paunch for the matter, and yet he would not be scrupulous — that is, he would not be wary."

Augurs are fortune-tellers who would examine the entrails of a sacrificed ox and then predict whether the future would be good or bad.

Tucca the military man said to Luscus:

"How is this now, goodman slave? What, roly poly? We are all rivals, rascal?"

A roly poly is a worthless person.

Tucca thought that Luscus, a servant, was trying to make himself the equal of Tucca and the others present.

Tucca was basically a beggar, and he was protective of what he regarded as his prerogatives. One way to build up yourself is to tear down others.

He then said to Ovid Senior:

"Why, my Master of Worship, do thou hear? Are these thy best projects?

"Is this thy designs and thy discipline, to allow knaves to be competitors with commanders and gentlemen?"

Tucca then said to Luscus:

"Are we parallels, rascal? Are we equals?"

Tucca, a beggar of sorts, considered himself to be better than Luscus, who was a servant and worked for a living.

Ovid Senior said to Luscus, "Sirrah, go and get my horses ready. You'll always be prating."

Tucca said to Luscus, "Do, you perpetual stinkard, do — go, talk to tapsters and ostlers, you slave; they are in your element — go; here are the Emperor's captains, you ragamuffin rascal, and not your comrades."

Tapsters are bartenders, and ostlers take care of horses.

Luscus exited.

Lupus the Tribune (a magistrate) said to Ovid Senior:

"Indeed, Marcus Ovid, these actors are an idle generation — that is, an idle breed — and do much harm in a state. They corrupt young gentry very much. I know it. I have not been a Tribune thus long and observed nothing.

"Besides, they will rob us, us who are magistrates, of our respect, bring us upon their stages by representing us and make us ridiculous to the plebeians; they will play you, or me, the wisest men they can come by, always — me! — only to bring us in contempt with the vulgar people and make us cheap."

The plebeians and the vulgar people were the common people. Patricians were the elite.

Lupus objected to being satirized in plays on stage.

Tucca said:

"Thee are in the right, my venerable cropshin — they will indeed."

A cropshin is an inferior herring.

Tucca continued:

"The tongue of the oracle never twanged truer."

Oracles prophesized; they did not twang.

Tucca continued:

"Your courtier cannot kiss his mistress' slippers in quiet because of them, nor can your white — that is, pure — innocent gallant pawn his reveling suit — his party outfit — to buy his punk a supper."

A punk is a prostitute.

Tucca, who was decayed (down on his luck) and whose honesty was questionable, continued:

"An honest decayed commander cannot skelder and con people, cheat, nor be seen in a bawdy house, but he shall immediately appear in one of their wormwood — bitter — comedies.

"They — the actors — are grown licentious, the rogues: They are libertines, complete libertines. They forget they are in the statute, the rascals."

By statute, actors could be charged with being rogues or vagabonds unless their acting troupe had a high-ranking member of society as its patron.

Tucca continued:

"They are blazoned there; there they are tricked, they and their pedigrees; they need no other heralds, to be sure.

A blazon is a detailed heraldic description of a coat of arms or other heraldic device. A tricked coat of arms is an outline of a coat of arms. The Heralds' College was authorized to issue coats of arms.

According to Tucca, the only kind of heralds that actors need is those who proclaim that the actors are scoundrels.

Ovid Senior said to his son the poet, "I think if nothing else, yet this alone, the reading of the public edicts against actors, should frighten thee away from commerce — contact — with them and give thee distaste enough of their actions. But this betrays what a student you are; this argues your 'proficiency' in the law."

He was arguing that his son in fact had contact with actors, so therefore his son was ignorant of or dismissive of the public edicts and so was a poor law student.

Ovid replied:

"They wrong me, sir, and do abuse you more, those who blow these untrue reports into your ears. I am not known to the open stage, nor do I traffic in their theaters."

An open stage is open for business, and/or it is a stage that is open to the elements — no roof.

Ovid continued:

"Indeed, I do acknowledge, at the request of some close friends and honorable Romans, I have begun a poem of that nature."

Ovid's poem was a play.

Ben Jonson considered himself a poet. He wrote poetry, and his plays contained verse as well as prose.

"You have, sir?" Ovid Senior said. "A poem? And where is it? Poetry is the 'law' you study."

"Cornelius Gallus borrowed it to read," Ovid replied.

Ovid Senior said:

"Cornelius Gallus? There's another gallant, fashionable gentleman, too, who has drunk of the same poison as you; and so have Tibullus, and Propertius.

"But these are gentlemen of means and revenue, now.

"In contrast, thou are a younger brother, and have nothing but thy bare exhibition, aka allowance or maintenance — which I protest shall be bare indeed if thou don't forsake these unprofitable by-courses, and that timely, too."

Under the principle of primogeniture, the oldest son inherited the bulk of the father's wealth. Younger sons inherited little or nothing.

Ovid Senior was threatening to cut down or cut off Ovid's allowance unless he stopped writing poetry.

Ovid Senior continued:

"Name me a professed poet whose poetry has ever afforded him so much as a competency: an adequate income.

"Aye, your god of poets there, whom all of you admire and reverence so much, Homer, he whose worm-eaten statue must not be spewed against — spit at — except with hallowed lips and groveling adoration, what was he? What was he?"

Tucca said to Ovid Senior, "By the Virgin Mary, I'll tell thee, old swaggerer and quarreler: He was a poor, blind, rhyming rascal, who lived obscurely up and down in booths — temporary dwellings — and taphouses, and scarcely ever got a good meal even in his dreams, the whoreson hungry beggar."

Actually, in Homer's *Odyssey*, the blind reciter of poetry, Demodocus, is well respected. After listening to him, Odysseus rewards him with the best cut of meat.

Homer's epic poems have poetic meter, but they do not rhyme.

Ovid Senior said to his son, Ovid:

"He says well.

"I know this nettles you, now, but answer me: Isn't it true? You'll tell me his name shall live, and that (now being dead) his works have eternalized him and made him divine. But could this divinity feed him while he lived? Could his name feast him?"

"Or purchase him a Senator's revenue?" Tucca asked. "Could it?"

Qualifying to be a Senator required much wealth.

The same was true of Knights in the Middle Ages.

Ovid Senior said, "Aye, or give him place — status — in the commonwealth? Respect or attendants? Make him be carried in his litter?"

Senators and other high-ranking people could be carried in litters.

Tucca said to Ovid Senior, "Thou speak sentences, old Bias."

Bias of Priene was a Greek sage; he was one of the Seven Sages.

"Sentences" are maxims. They can be wise.

Lupus said to Ovid, "All this the law will do, young sir, if you'll follow it."

In other words: To be successful, be a lawyer; to be a failure, be a poet.

Ovid Senior said, "If he is my son, he shall follow and observe what I will make him fit for, or I profess here openly and utterly to disown him."

Ovid replied:

"Sir, let me ask that you will forgo these moods.

"I will be anything, or study anything; I'll show that the unfashioned body of the law is pure elegance, and make her ruggedest strains run as smoothly as Propertius' elegies."

"Propertius' elegies?" Ovid Senior said sarcastically. "Good!"

"Nay, you take — judge — your son too quickly, Marcus," Lupus said to Ovid Senior.

"Why, he cannot speak, he cannot think, out of poetry," Ovid Senior said. "He is bewitched with it."

"Come, do not misprize him," Lupus responded.

"Misprize" means "undervalue." As a legal term, it means to commit a wrongful act or a wrongful omission.

Ovid Senior said, "'Misprize'? Aye, by the Virgin Mary, I would have him use some such words, now; they have some touch, some taste, of the law. He should make himself a style out of these, and let his Propertius' elegies go by."

Lupus said:

"Indeed, young Publius, he who will now hit the mark must shoot through the law; we have no other planet that reigns, and in that sphere you may sit and sing with angels."

Young Publius is young Ovid the poet, son of Ovid Senior.

In the medieval view of the cosmos, the Sun, planets and stars were encased in Spheres that revolved around the Earth. The outermost Sphere was the Primum Mobile, which moved and imparted movement to the other Spheres of the cosmos, and that movement caused the Music of the Spheres, something that living human beings normally do not hear.

Angels are also English coins. A person with many angels may very well sing.

Lupus continued:

"Why, the law makes a man happy without respecting and paying heed to any other merit; a simple, undistinguished scholar, or none at all, may be a lawyer."

Tucca said to Ovid:

"He tells thee true, my noble neophyte; my little grammaticaster, he does."

A grammaticaster is a pedantic grammarian.

Tucca continued:

"Law shall never put thee to and make thee work at thy mathematics, metaphysics, philosophy, and I don't know what other supposed sufficiencies and accomplishments. If thou can but have the patience to plod enough, talk enough, and make noise enough, then be impudent enough, and it is enough."

"Three books will furnish you," Lupus said.

Tucca said:

"And the less art, the better.

"Besides, when it shall be in the power of thy cheverel — flexible — conscience to do right or wrong at thy pleasure, my pretty Alcibiades —"

Alcibiades was a gifted Athenian, but he sometimes fought for and sometimes fought against Athens during the Peloponnesian War that pitted Sparta against Athens. Ovid preferred poetry, but he was considering turning to law to please his father.

Lupus interrupted, "Aye, and to have better men than himself, by many thousand degrees, to observe him and stand bare —"

Tucca interrupted, "True, and he to carry himself proud and stately, and have the law on his side for it, old boy."

Ovid Senior said to his friends:

"Well, the day grows old, gentlemen, and I must leave you."

He then said to his son the poet:

"Publius, if thou will hold my favor, abandon these idle, fruitless studies that so bewitch thee. Send Janus home his back-face again and look only forward to the law: Focus on that. I will allow thee what allowance shall suit thee in the rank of gentlemen and shall maintain thy society with the best; and under these conditions I leave thee."

Janus is a two-faced god who looks both forwards and backwards. Ovid Senior wanted his son, Ovid, to stop looking at poetry and instead look only at law.

Ovid Senior continued:

"My blessings will light upon thee if thou respect these conditions; if not, my eyes may drop tears for thee, but thine own heart will ache for itself; and so farewell."

Luscus returned.

Ovid Senior asked him, "Are my horses ready?"

"Yes, sir, they are at the gate outside," Luscus answered.

"That's well," Ovid Senior said.

He then said, "Asinius Lupus, let me have a word with you."

He then said to Tucca, "Captain, shall I take my leave of you?"

"No, my little old boy," Tucca said.

He motioned toward Lupus and said to Ovid Senior, "Dispatch your business with Cothurnus there."

A cothernus is a thick-soled boot that was worn by actors, such as those playing important men of state. Lupus considered himself an important man of state.

Tucca continued, "I'll wait on thee, I will."

Luscus said to himself, "To borrow some ten drachmas; I know his project."

Tucca's project was to get money from Ovid Senior and then spend it.

Ovid Senior said to Lupus, "Sir, you shall make me beholden to you."

He then asked, "Now, Captain Tucca, what do you have to say?"

Tucca answered:

"Why, what should I say? Or what can I say, my flower of the Equestrian order?"

The Equestrian order was Knights, who were just below the highest order: the Nobles.

Tucca continued:

"Should I say thou are rich? Or that thou are honorable? Or wise? Or valiant? Or learned? Or liberal?

"Why, thou are all these, and thou know it, my noble Lucullus, thou know it; come, don't be ashamed of thy virtues, old stump."

Lucullus was a retired general and a wealthy patron of soldiers.

The word "stump" can refer to a short man or a blockhead.

Tucca continued:

"Honor's a good brooch — metaphorical ornament — to wear in a man's hat at all times. Thou are the man of war's Maecenas, old boy."

Maecenas was a friend to Augustus Caesar, and he was an important patron of the arts.

Tucca wanted Ovid Senior to be a patron of military men.

Tucca continued:

"Why shouldn't thou be graced then by the men of war as well as he is by his poets?"

A Pyrgus entered the room. An assistant in Tucca's cons, he had been waiting in the anteroom and listening for his cue to enter and assist in a con.

A Pyrgus is literally a tall, moveable structure used in sieges. Here, it is a joke name for Tucca's short boy-pages.

Tucca said to the Pyrgus, "What is it now, my carrier? What is the news?"

The Pyrgus whispered to Tucca.

Luscus said to himself, "The boy has stayed within for his cue this half hour."

Tucca said out loud to the Pyrgus, "Come, do not whisper to me, but speak it out. What? It is no treason against the state, I hope, is it?"

"Yes, against the state of my master's purse," Luscus said to himself.

"Sir, Agrippa desires you to be patient with him until the next week," the Pyrgus said. "His moils are not yet come up."

Agrippa is Augustus Caesar's son-in-law and a wealthy military commander. Tucca will say that Agrippa owes him nearly a talent, which is thousands of British pounds or USAmerican dollars.

The Pyrgus was using the word "moils" to mean mules. The verb "moil" means "work hard."

Tucca said:

"His moils?

"Now the bots, the spavin, and the glanders, and some dozen more diseases alight on him and his moils! What! Have they the yellow jaundice, his moils, that they come no faster? Or are they foundered and lame, huh? His moils have the staggers, likely, haven't they?"

Tucca had named several diseases Agrippa's mules might be suffering from.

The Pyrgus replied, "Oh, no, sir."

He then said to himself, "Then your tongue might be suspected for one of his moils."

Tucca stuttered and sputtered when angry — or when he pretended to be angry.

Tucca said out loud so that Ovid Senior could hear him:

"He owes me almost a talent, and he thinks to bear it away — a victory for him — with his moils, does he?"

He then said to the Pyrgus:

"Sirrah, you nutcracker, go on your way to him again, and tell him I must have money, I."

"Nutcrackers" are apprentices who like to crack nuts while attending a play.

Tucca continued:

"I cannot eat stones and turfs, tell him.

"What! Will he clem — starve — me and my followers? Ask him if he will clem me; do, go. He would have me fry my jacket and eat it, would he?

"Away, setter, away.

"Yet stay, my little tumbler."

Setters and tumblers are hunting dogs. The Pyrgus was supposed to hunt for Agrippa.

The words are also slang words for assistants to conmen. A setter finds people who can be conned. A tumbler leads the victims to the conman.

Tucca motioned to Ovid Senior and said quietly to the Pyrgus, "This old boy shall supply money now."

He said out loud, "I will not trouble Agrippa, I cannot be importunate, I; I cannot be impudent to him."

"Alas, sir, no," the Pyrgus said. "You are the most maidenly, blushing creature upon the earth."

Tucca said to Ovid Senior, "Do thou hear, my little six-and-fifty or thereabouts? Thou are not to learn the humors and tricks of that old bald cheater, Time; thou had not this chain for nothing."

A chain can be worn as a necklace or as a symbol of authority.

Tucca was flattering Ovid Senior by telling him that he was a mature and knowledgeable man.

Time is bald. Once a moment is past, it cannot be possessed again. Time has no long hair that you can grab as Time passes by you.

Tucca continued: "Men of worth have their chimeras as well as other creatures; and they see monsters sometimes; they do, they do, brave boy."

Chimeras were mythological monsters that were made of parts of various animals. The parts vary in different descriptions, but often the chimera is described as having a lion's head, a goat's body, and a serpent's tail.

The Pyrgus said to himself, "At cheaper cost than if he — Tucca — shall see you, I warrant him."

It's better to have a chimera see you than to have Tucca see you.

Tucca said quietly to Ovid Senior, "Thou must let me have six, six —
drachmas, I mean, old boy; thou shall do it; I tell thee, old boy, thou shall, and
in private, too, do thou see? Go, walk off."

Whenever Tucca mentioned a number, he had to think about what was
the greatest amount of money he could get from a person. Should he ask for
shillings, or for drachmas, or for sesterces?

He pointed and said, "There, there. Six is the sum. Thy son's a gallant spark
and must not be put out suddenly."

Ovid Senior went to the side to search his pockets for money to give to
Tucca.

Tucca then said to young Ovid, "Come here, Callimachus."

Callimachus was a poet who inspired Ovid.

Tucca continued:

"Thy father tells me thou are too poetical, boy; thou must not be so, thou
must leave them — leave the poets — young novice, thou must.

"They are a sort of poor, starved rascals, who are always wrapped up in foul
linen — dirty clothing — and can boast of nothing but a lean visage peering
out of a seam-rent — torn at the seams — suit: the very emblems and signs of
beggary.

"No, do thou hear? Turn lawyer, thou shall be my solicitor —"

Tucca was providing a kind of service for his six drachmas. He had given
young Ovid the same advice that Ovid Senior had given. He had also advised
Ovid Senior to go a little easy on his son: Don't put out his son — and his son's
spark — suddenly.

Ovid Senior returned with money for Tucca.

Tucca asked Ovid Senior, "It is the right amount, old boy, isn't it?"

"You had best tell — count — it, Captain," Ovid Senior said.

"No," Tucca said. "Fare thou well, my honest horseman."

A horseman is 1) a person who rides a horse, or 2) a member of the
Equestrian social rank — a Knight.

Tucca then said to Lupus, "And fare thou well, beaver."

Beaver hats were expensive hats worn by gentlemen.

Tucca said to Ovid Senior:

"I ask thee, Roman, when thou come to town, see me at my lodging and
visit me sometimes. Thou shall be welcome, old boy. Do not balk — avoid and

disappoint — me, good swaggerer. May Jove keep thy chain from having to be pawned.

"Go thy ways; if thou lack money, I'll lend thee some; I'll leave thee to thy horse, now. Adieu."

"Farewell, good Captain," Ovid Senior said.

Tucca said quietly to the Pyrgus, "Boy, you can have but half a share now, boy."

He meant half of the Pyrgus' share in the profits of the con. Tucca owed everybody, including his pages.

Tucca and the Pyrgus exited.

Ovid Senior said, "It is a strange boldness that accompanies this fellow."

Did Ovid Senior know he had been conned? Possibly. He could afford the loss of the "loan."

"Come," Ovid Senior said to Luscus.

Ovid said, "I'll give attendance on you to your horse, sir, if it pleases you —"

His father replied, "No; stay in your chamber and fall to your studies. Do so; may the gods of Rome bless thee!"

Ovid Senior, Lupus, and Luscus exited, leaving Ovid the poet alone.

Ovid the poet said to himself:

"And may the gods give me stomach to digest this law — those are the words that should have surely followed his words, had I been he.

"O sacred poesy, thou spirit of arts, the soul of science and the queen of souls, what profane violence, almost sacrilege, has here been offered to thy divinities!

"That thine own guiltless poverty should arm Prodigious Ignorance to wound thee thus!

"For from poets' poverty is all the force of argument drawn forth against poesy, or from the abuse of thy great powers in adulterated and corrupted brain."

In other words: The major complaint many people make against poetry is that poets tend to be poor in wealth.

Ovid the poet continued:

"But if men would only learn to distinguish spirits, and to set and acknowledge a true difference between those jaded wits who run a broken pace of poetic meter for common hire, and the high raptures of a happy muse borne on the wings of her immortal thought that kicks at earth with a disdainful heel and beats at the gates of heaven with her bright hooves, they would not then with such distorted faces and desperate censures stab at poesy."

Bad poets are like jades: inferior horses. Good poets are like Pegasus: a winged horse that ascends the heavens.

Ovid the poet continued:

"Men would then admire bright knowledge, and their minds should never descend on so unworthy objects as gold or titles; they would dread far more to be thought ignorant than to be known poor.

"The time was once, when wit drowned wealth; but now your only barbarism is to have wit, and want.

"No matter now who excels in virtue, he who has coin has all perfection else."

In other words: Many men think that it is better to be wealthy and stupid than to be intelligent and impoverished.

Tibullus, a poet and one of Ovid's friends, entered the scene and said, "Ovid?"

"Who's there?" Ovid asked.

Seeing Tibullus, he said, "Come in."

"Good morning, lawyer," Tibullus said.

"Good morning, dear Tibullus," Ovid said. "Welcome. Sit down."

"Not I," Tibullus said. "What, so hard at it?"

He approached Ovid, who attempted to withhold his work.

Tibullus said, "Let's see, what's here? Nay, I will see it —"

"Please, stay away," Ovid said.

They struggled, but Tibullus got hold of the paper.

Tibullus read Ovid's writing out loud:

"If thrice in field a man vanquish his foe,

"'Tis after in his choice to serve, or no."

The man is a soldier, and if he vanquishes three enemies on the battlefield, it is his decision whether he continues to serve as a soldier or goes home.

"What is this now, Ovid!" Tibullus said. "Law-cases in verse?"

"In truth, I don't know," Ovid said. "They run from my pen unwittingly, if they are verse."

Ovid wrote verse whether he intended to or not. He couldn't help it.

He then asked, "What's the news in the outside world?"

"Off with this lawyer gown you are wearing!" Tibullus said. "I have come to have thee walk with me."

Tibullus wanted Ovid to cease his study of law and do something different and, no doubt, more fun.

Ovid replied, "No, good Tibullus, I'm not now in case — I'm not now in a position to do that. Please leave me alone."

"What! Not in case?" Tibullus said. "By God's light, thou are in too much case, judging by all this law."

Ovid's room contained law books and his notes about the law.

"Truly, if I live, I will new-dress the law in sprightly poesy's habiliments," Ovid said.

"The hell thou will!" Tibullus said. "What, turn law into verse? Thy father has schooled thee, I see."

He took out a letter, which he handed to Ovid.

Tibullus then said, "Here, read that. There's subject for you — and, if I mistake not, a *supersedeas* to your melancholy."

A *supersedeas* is a writ for a stay in proceedings.

In other words, the letter would cheer Ovid up.

Ovid opened the letter and said, "What! Signed 'Julia'! O my life, my heaven!"

He read the letter silently to himself.

"Has your mood changed?" Tibullus asked.

Ovid said about the letter's contents, "Music of wit! Note for the harmonious spheres!"

The note was 1) a musical note, and 2) Julia's letter to Ovid.

He added, "Celestial accents, how you ravish me!"

"Accents" can be 1) utterances, and 2) marks on musical notes.

"What is it, Ovid?" Tibullus asked.

"That I must meet my Julia, the Princess Julia," Ovid said.

"Where?" Tibullus asked.

"Why, at — by the Heart of God, I have forgotten," Ovid said. "My passion — my strong emotion — so transports me."

"I'll save your trouble of trying to remember," Tibullus said. "It is at Albius' house, the jeweler's, where the fair Lycoris lies."

"Who? Cytheris, Cornelius Gallus' love?" Ovid asked.

"Aye, he'll be there, too, and my Plautia," Tibullus said.

"And why not your Delia?" Ovid asked.

"Yes, and your Corinna," Tibullus said.

Both Ovid and Tibullus wrote poetry about the women they loved; in their poetry they used pseudonyms for their loved ones.

Ovid loved Julia, and he wrote about her in his poetry, using the name Corinna.

Tibullus loved Plautia, and he wrote about her in his poetry, using the name Delia.

Ovid said:

"True, but my sweet Tibullus, keep that secret.

"I would not for all Rome have it thought that I veil bright Julia underneath that name: Julia, the gem and jewel — the Jule — of my soul, who takes her honors from the golden sky, as beauty takes all its luster from her eye.

"The air respires and breathes out again the pure Elysian — heavenly — sweets in which she breathes, and from her looks descend the glories of the summer. Heaven she is, praised in herself above all praise — Julia is more praiseworthy than any words that could be used to praise her — and he who hears her speak would swear the tuneful orbs — the musical Spheres — turned in his zenith only."

In other words: Anyone who hears Julia speak thinks that he is hearing the Music of the Spheres.

"Publius, thou shall lose thyself," Tibullus said.

Publius Ovid replied:

"Oh, in no labyrinth can I safelier err than when I lose myself in praising her.

"Go away from here, law, and welcome, Muses! Though you Muses are not rich, yet you are pleasing; let's be reconciled and now made one.

"Henceforth I promise you my faith, and I promise all my serious hours to spend with you — with you, whose music strikes on my heart and with bewitching tones steals forth my spirit in Julia's name. Fair Julia!

"Julia's love shall be a law, and that sweet law I'll study: the law and art of sacred Julia's love.

"All other objects will prove to be only abjects — abject objects."

"Come, we shall have thee as passionate as Propertius soon," Tibullus said.

"Oh, how does my Sextus?" Ovid asked about Sextus Propertius.

"Truly, he is full of sorrow for his Cynthia's death," Tibullus answered.

"What, still?" Ovid asked.

"Still, and still more," Tibullus said. "His griefs grow upon him as do his hours. Never did I know an understanding spirit so take to heart the common — universal — work of fate."

Ovid said:

"O my Tibullus, let us not blame him, for against such occurrences the heartiest strife of virtue is not proof.

"We may preach constancy and fortitude to other souls, but had we ourselves been struck with the like planet, one with malign influences — had our loves, like his, been ravished from us by injurious death, and in the height and heat of our best days — it would have cracked our sinews, shrunk our veins, and made our very heartstrings jar and go out of tune, like his."

Ben Jonson's society believed that planets could influence our lives, and it believed that strings brace the heart, and that those strings could break. The figurative sense of "heartstrings" is one's deepest feelings, such as passionate love.

Ovid continued:

"Come, let's go and take him forth, and see if mirth or company will but abate — lessen — his passion."

"I am happy to do so," Tibullus said, "and I implore the gods that it may."

They exited.

CHAPTER 2

— 2.1 —

Albius and Crispinus talked together.

Albius was a tradesman, primarily a jeweler, who was married to Chloe.

Crispinus was a poetaster — a bad poet — who was carrying a folded sheet of paper.

Albius said:

"Master Crispinus, you are welcome. Please use a stool, sir."

Stools were used to sit on in polite company. They were also used in to sit on in privies.

Albius continued:

"Your cousin Cytheris will come down soon. We are so busy for the receiving of these courtiers here that I can scarcely be a minute alone with myself because of thinking about them.

"Please sit, sir; please sit, sir."

"I am very well, sir," Crispinus said. "Never trust me but you are most delicately seated here, full of sweet delight and blandishment! An excellent air, an excellent air!"

By "blandishment," Crispinus meant "allurement."

Albius had a nice house in a nice location.

"Aye, sir, it is a pretty air," Albius said.

He then said to himself, "These courtiers run in my mind still; I must look out —"

He then said to Crispinus, "For Jupiter's sake, sit, sir. Or will it please you to walk into the garden? There's a garden at the back side of the house — in the backyard."

Jupiter is the King of the gods.

"I am most strenuously well, I thank you, sir," Crispinus said.

"May it do you much good, sir," Albius said.

He exited.

Chloe, Albius' wife, entered with some maids who were carrying perfume and dried herbs to sweeten the air of the house.

Choe, who did not notice Crispinus, said to her maids, "Come, bring those perfumes forward a little, and strew some roses and violets here."

Albius entered the room.

Chloe noticed Albius.

Chloe said, "Bah, here are rooms that savor — stink — the most pitifully rank that ever I felt!"

Of course, she meant "smelled."

She then said, "I cry the gods mercy, my husband's in the wind of us."

In other words, her husband stank.

Albius said to his wife, "Why, this is good, excellent, excellent. Well done, my sweet Chloe. Trim up your house most obsequiously — dutifully, and eager to please."

"For Vulcan's sake, breathe somewhere else!" Chloe said. "In truth, you overcome our perfumes exceedingly; you are too predominant."

Vulcan, the gifted blacksmith god, was, like Albius, married; in fact, he was married to Venus, goddess of beauty and sexual passion, who was not faithful to him. Venus had an affair with Mars, the god of war. Vulcan learned of the affair, so he set a trap for the illicit lovers. He created a fine net that bound tightly, he placed the net above his bed, and then he pretended to leave his mansion to journey abroad. Mars ran to Venus, and together they ran to bed. Mars and Venus lay down in bed together, and then the fine net snared them, locked in lust.

"Just hear my opinion, sweet wife," Albius said.

He tried to hug her and pin her in his arms, but she fended him off and hit him on the head.

Chloe said:

"A pin for your 'pinion."

A pin is an almost worthless small item used in sewing.

Chloe continued:

"In sincerity, if you are thus fulsome — offensive — to me in everything, I'll be divorced. God save my body! You know what you were before I married you. I was a gentlewoman born, I. I lost all my friends to be a citizen's wife, because I heard, indeed, that they kept their wives as fine as ladies, and that we might rule our husbands like ladies, and do whatever we wanted.

"Do you think I would have married you otherwise?"

Albius said, "I acknowledge, sweet wife —"

He then whispered to Crispinus, "She speaks the best of any woman in Italy, and moves as mightily, which makes me prefer that she should make bumps on my head as big as my two fingers than I would offend her."

"Moves ... mightily" can mean "persuades well in speech" or "strikes hard with her fist."

When Albius mentioned "two fingers," he held up two fingers.

In this society, cuckolds — men with unfaithful wives — were said to have invisible horns growing on their heads. Readers may be forgiven for thinking of those horns when Albius held up two fingers.

He then said to Chloe, "But, sweet wife —"

"Yet again?" his wife said. "Isn't it grace enough for you that I call you husband and you call me wife, but you must still be poking me against my will to things?"

One kind of poking is sexual poking. One meaning of "thing" is "penis."

Albius replied, "But you know, wife: Here are the greatest ladies and most gallant gentlemen of Rome to be entertained in our house now; and I would like to advise thee to entertain them in the best sort, indeed, wife."

Chloe said:

"In sincerity, did you ever hear a man talk so idly? You would seem to be the master of me? You would have your spoke in my cart?"

Hmm. There's a sexual meaning there.

Chloe continued:

"You would advise me to entertain ladies and gentlemen? Because you can marshal your pack needles, horse combs, hobbyhorses, and wall candlesticks in your warehouse better than I, therefore you can tell how to entertain ladies and gentlefolks better than I?"

Albius said:

"O my sweet wife, don't upbraid me with that!

"'Gain savors sweetly from anything.'"

"Gain" is profit.

Albius continued:

"He who respects" — he meant "expects" — "to get a profit must relish all commodities alike, and admit no difference between woad [a plant used to make blue dye] and frankincense, or the most precious balsamum and a tar barrel."

Albius was a tradesman who dealt in jewelry, but he also dealt in other less prestigious items that made a profit.

Chloe said:

"By the Virgin Mary, bah!

"You sell candle-snuffers, too, if you remember, but I ask you to let me buy them out of your hand, for I tell you true, I take it highly in snuff — I highly resent — to learn how to entertain gentlefolks by your instruction at these years of mine, indeed.

"Alas, man, there was not a gentleman who came to your house in your other wife's time, I think? Nor a lady? Nor one or more musicians? Nor masques?"

Masques were entertainments at which people wore masks.

Chloe continued:

"Neither you, nor your house were so much as spoken of before I disbased myself from my hood and my fartingale to these bum-rolls and your whalebone bodice."

By "disbased," she meant "debased."

Before becoming a tradesman's wife, she had worn a French hood and a farthingale (not a "fartingale").

After becoming a tradesman's wife, she wore the items of clothing usually worn by a tradesman's wife: Bum-rolls were rolls of cloth around the hips; a skirt was draped over them. A whalebone bodice was a bodice stiffened with whalebone.

Albius said:

"Look here, my sweet wife."

He lay his finger on his lips and said:

"I am mum, my dear mummia, my balsamum, my spermaceti, and my very city of —"

Hmm. My very city of ... sperm? Yes. He was still referring to his wife. A city is a site.

Mummia, balsamum, and spermaceti are expensive items.

Mummia is a medicinal preparation made from the preserved flesh of a mummy.

Balsamum is aromatic resin used as an ointment.

Spermaceti is a waxy substance produced in sperm whales; it was used as an ointment.

Albius then said quietly to Crispinus, "She has the most best, true, feminine wit in Rome!"

Crispinus replied, "I have heard so, sir, and do most vehemently desire to participate" — he meant "partake of" — "the knowledge of her fair features."

"Ah, peace," Albius said. "You shall hear more soon; be not seen yet, please — not yet. Observe."

He exited.

Chloe said, "By God's body, give husbands the head a little more, and they'll be nothing but head shortly."

To give a horse the head means to loosen the reins and give it freedom. If Chloe gives her husband the head, soon he will be her head — her boss.

Ephesians 5:23 states, *"For the husband is the head of the wife, even as Christ is the head of the church: and he is the saviour of the body"* (King James Bible).

Chloe, who had noticed her husband talking to Crispinus, motioned toward him and asked her maids, "Who's he there?"

"I don't know, forsooth," the first maid said.

"Forsooth" means "indeed" or "in truth."

The second maid asked Crispinus, "Who would you speak with, sir?"

He answered, "I would speak with my cousin Cytheris."

The second maid said to Chloe, "He is one, forsooth, who would speak with his cousin Cytheris."

"Is she your cousin, sir?" Chloe asked.

"Yes, in truth, forsooth, for lack of a better," Crispinus said.

For lack of a better cousin.

"Is she a gentlewoman?" Chloe asked.

"Or else she should not be my cousin, I assure you," Crispinus said.

"Are you a gentleman born?" Chloe asked.

"That I am, lady," Crispinus said. "You shall see my arms, if it will please you."

"No, your legs do sufficiently show you are a gentleman born, sir; for a man borne upon little legs is always a gentleman borne," Chloe said.

"Yet I ask you, permit me to show you the sight of my arms, mistress," Crispinus said, "for I bear them about me, to have them seen."

Yes, bare arms can be seen.

He pulled out a design of a coat of arms and held it up.

He then said:

"My name is Crispinus, or Cry-spinas, indeed, which is well expressed in my arms: a face crying, in chief; and beneath it a bloody toe between three thorns pungent."

Spina is Latin for "thorn."

"In chief" means the top part of the shield.

"Pungent" means "sharp-pointed" (the thorns) and "stinky" (the toe).

"Then you are welcome, sir," Chloe said. "Now that I know you are a gentleman born, I can find in my heart to welcome you; for I am a gentlewoman born, too, and I will bear my head high enough, although it were my fortune to marry a tradesman."

Crispinus replied, "No doubt of that, sweet feature" — he may have meant "creature" — "your carriage shows it in any man's eye that is carried upon you with judgment."

"Carriage " can mean bodily deportment as well as a kind of wheeled vehicle.

By "carried," he meant "cast."

Albius returned. In the next few minutes, he would be continually going in and out of the room. He really, really wanted to make a good impression on the VIPs coming to his home.

"Dear wife, don't be angry," he said.

"God's my passion!" Chloe said.

"Listen to me about one thing," Albius said. "Don't let your maids set cushions in the parlor windows, nor in the dining-chamber windows, nor upon stools in either of them, in any case, for it is tavern-like; but lay them one upon another in some outer-room or corner of the dining chamber."

"Go, go," Chloe said. "Meddle with your bedchamber only, or rather with your bed in your chamber only, or rather with your wife in your bed only; or, on my faith, I'll not be pleased with you only."

Hmm. Sounds as if someone will shortly be a cuckold.

Albius said, "Look here, my dear wife, entertain that gentleman kindly, I ask you —"

Chloe made a gesture as if she were going to hit him.

Albius lay his finger on his lips and said, "Mum."

That meant, he would stay quiet.

"Go! I need your instruction, indeed!" Chloe said sarcastically.

She added, without sarcasm, "Anger me no more, I advise you."

Albius exited.

Chloe said to herself, "City-sin, did he say! She's a wise gentlewoman, indeed, who will marry herself to the sin of the city."

"City-sin" is a citizen. The "sin of the city" is something different.

Albius entered the room and said, "Just this one time and no more, by heaven, wife. Hang no pictures in the hall nor in the dining chamber, in any case, but in the gallery only, for it is not courtly else, on my word, wife."

Chloe replied, "By God's precious, are you never done!"

Albius said, "Wife —"

She raised her fist and threatened to hit him.

He exited.

Chloe asked, "Don't I bear a reasonable corrigible hand over him, Crispinus?"

"Corrigible" means "corrective."

Crispinus replied, "By this hand, lady, you hold a most sweet hand over him."

Albius entered the room and said, "And then for the great gilt andirons —"

"Again!" Chloe said. "I wish that the andirons were in your great guts, as far as I'm concerned."

"I vanish, wife," Albius said.

He exited.

Chloe asked:

"What shall I do, Master Crispinus?

"Here will be all the most splendid ladies in court soon, to see your cousin Cytheris. O the gods! How might I behave myself now so as to entertain them most courtly?"

Crispinus answered, "By the Virgin Mary, lady, if you will entertain them most courtly, you must do thus:

"As soon as ever your maid or your man brings you word they have come, you must say, 'A pox on them! What are they doing here?'

"And yet when they come, speak to them as fair words as can be and give them the kindest welcome in words that can be."

"Is that the fashion of courtiers, Crispinus?" Chloe asked.

"I assure you it is, lady," Crispinus said. "I have observed it."

Chloe said, "As for your 'pox,' sir, it is easily hit on; but it is not so easy to speak fair after, I think?"

The pox is syphilis, which is easily hit on, or acquired. Once one learns that it has been acquired, one is unlikely to say fair words.

Albius entered the room and said, "Oh, wife, the coaches have come, on my word, a number of coaches, and courtiers."

"A pox on them!" Chloe said. "What are they doing here?"

"What is this now, wife!" Albius said. "Would thou not have them come?"

"Come?" Chloe replied. "Come, you are a fool, you."

She then said to Crispinus, "He doesn't know the trick of it."

In other words, he doesn't understand courtly etiquette.

Chloe then ordered her maids, "Call Cytheris, please."

A maid exited.

Chloe then said, "And good Master Crispinus, you can observe, you say; let me entreat you for all the ladies' behaviors, jewels, jests, and attires, that you marking as well as I, we may put both our marks together when they are gone, and confer about them."

A mark is a close observation, or an object. Chloe was unintentionally talking about putting two sexual objects together.

"I assure you, sweet lady, that I do so," Crispinus said. "Let me alone to observe until I turn myself to nothing but observation."

Cytheris entered the room.

Crispinus said, "Good morning, cousin Cytheris."

"Welcome, kind cousin," Cytheris said. "What! Have they come?"

"Aye, your friend Cornelius Gallus, Ovid, Tibullus, Propertius, with Julia the Emperor's daughter and the lady Plautia, have alighted at the door, and with them Hermogenes Tigellius, the excellent musician."

Julia was the daughter of Augustus Caesar, the Roman Emperor.

"Come, let us go meet them, Chloe," Cytheris said.

"Observe them, Crispinus," Chloe said.

"At a hair's breadth, lady, I assure you," Crispinus said. "I will very closely observe them."

<h1 style="text-align:center">— 2.2 —</h1>

Gallus, Ovid, Tibullus, Propertius, Hermogenes the musician, Julia, and Plautia entered the scene.

Ovid loved Julia, and Tibullus loved Plautia.

Gallus kissed Chloe and said, "Health to the lovely Chloe!"

He then said to Cytheris, "You must pardon me, mistress, that I give preference to this fair gentlewoman."

A mistress is a woman to whom a man is devoted. The word "mistress" need not imply a sexual liaison.

Gallus and the other guests do and will show much courtesy to Chloe, who is much concerned about social rank.

"I pardon and praise you for it, sir —" Cytheris said.

She then said to Julia, "— and I beseech Your Excellence, receive her beauties into your knowledge and favor."

Julia replied, "Cytheris, she has favor — good looks — and behavior that commands as much of me; and, sweet Chloe, know that I do exceedingly love you, and that I will approve of and second any grace that my father the Emperor may show you."

She motioned toward Albius and asked, "Is this your husband?"

"For lack of a better, if it pleases Your Highness," Albius said.

Chloe said to Cytheris, "God's my life! How he shames me!"

Cytheris replied, "Not a whit, Chloe; they all think you politic and witty; wise women don't choose husbands for the eye, merit, or birth, but for wealth and sovereignty."

"Sovereignty" in this context means "rule." Wise women choose husbands who are wealthy and whom they can rule over — or in some cases, when they prefer it, who will rule over them.

Ovid said to Albius, "Sir, we all come to congratulate you for the good report of you."

Tibullus said to Albius, "And we would be glad to deserve your love, sir."

Albius replied, "My wife will answer you all, gentlemen. I'll come to you again soon."

He exited.

Plautia motioned toward Chloe and said, "You have chosen for yourself a very fair companion here, Cytheris, and a very fair house."

"To both of which you and all my friends are very welcome, Plautia," Cytheris said.

These were words that should be spoken by the hostess, who was Chloe. Cytheris was a lodger.

Chloe, the real hostess, said, "With all my heart, I assure Your Ladyship."

"Thanks, sweet Mistress Chloe," Plautia said.

"You must come to court, lady, indeed, and there be sure your welcome shall be as great to us," Julia said to Chloe. "You will be as welcome to us as we are to you."

Ovid said to Julia, "She will well deserve it, madam. I see even in her looks gentry and general worthiness."

"I have not seen a more certain token of an excellent disposition," Tibullus said.

Albius returned and said, "Wife."

Chloe said to her husband, "Oh, they do so commend me here, the courtiers! What's the matter now?"

"For the banquet, sweet wife," Albius answered.

The banquet consisted of light refreshments: fruit, sweets, and wine.

"Yes," Chloe said. "And I must come to court, and be welcome, the princess says."

She and her husband exited.

Now that the respectable host and hostess were gone, Gallus said, "Ovid and Tibullus, you may be bold to welcome your mistresses here."

The couples embraced.

"We find it so, sir," Ovid said.

"And we thank Cornelius Gallus," Tibullus said.

Ovid said to Propertius, "Nay, my sweet Sextus, in faith, thou are not sociable."

"In faith, I am not, Publius, nor can I be," Sextus Propertius replied. "Sick minds are like sick men who burn with fevers, who, when they drink, are pleased with the taste for a moment, but afterward endure a more impatient fit."

He then said to all present, "Please, let me leave you; I offend you all, and myself most."

"Wait, sweet Propertius!" Gallus said.

"You yield too much to your griefs and fate, which never hurts except when we say it hurts us," Tibullus said.

The Stoic philosophers believed that suffering could be avoided by not acknowledging it.

Propertius said:

"Oh, peace, Tibullus!

"Your philosophy lends you too rough a hand to probe my wounds. Let they who know how to sigh and grieve speak about griefs. The free and unconstrained spirit does not feel the weight of my oppression."

Propertius exited.

"Worthy Roman!" Ovid said. "I think I taste his misery, and I could sit down and chide at his malignant stars."

"I think I love him because he loves so truly," Julia said.

Cytheris said, "This is the most perfect love — one that lives after death."

"Such is the constant ground of virtue always," Gallus said.

"It puts on an inseparable face," Plautia said.

Chloe returned, and she and Crispinus talked together apart from the others.

"Have you closely observed everything, Crispinus?" Chloe asked.

"Everything, I promise you," Crispinus said.

"What gentlemen are these?" Chloe asked. "Do you know them?"

"Aye, they are poets, lady," Crispinus said.

"Poets?" Chloe said. "They did not talk about me since I left, did they?"

"Oh, yes, and extolled your perfections to the heavens," Crispinus said.

"Now, in sincerity, they are the finest kind of men whomever I knew," Chloe said. "Poets! Couldn't one get the Emperor to make my husband a poet, do you think?"

"No, lady, it is love and beauty that make poets," Crispinus said, "and since you like poets so well, your love and beauties shall make me a poet."

"What! Shall they?" Chloe said. "And such a one as these?"

"Aye, and a better one than these," Crispinus said. "I would be sorry else."

"And shall your looks change? And your hair change? And all, like these?" Chloe asked.

"Why, a man may be a poet and yet not change his hair, lady," Crispinus said.

"Well, we shall see your cunning; yet if you can change your hair, please do," Chloe said.

Girls changed hairstyles when they became women, so why shouldn't men change hairstyles when they became poets?

Really, a haircut can help make a person look like the popular image of a poet, but of course, a good poet can look different from the popular image of a poet.

Albius returned and said, "Ladies and lordings, there's a slight banquet that awaits within for you; please draw near and accost it."

"We thank you, good Albius," Julia said. "But when shall we see those excellent jewels you are praised for having?"

One meaning of the word "jewels" is "testicles."

Albius said, "At Your Ladyship's service."

He then said to himself, "I got that speech by seeing a play yesterday, and it did me some grace now. I see it is good to collect such quotations sometimes. I'll frequent these plays more than I have done, now that I come to be familiar with courtiers."

Gallus approached Hermogenes and asked, "Why, how are you now, Hermogenes? What? Do thou ail, I wonder?"

"I am a little melancholy," Hermogenes said. "Let me alone, I ask thee."

"Melancholy!" Gallus said. "Why so?"

"With riding," Hermogenes said. "A plague on all coaches for me!"

Chloe pointed to Hermogenes and asked, "Is that hard-favored — scowling — gentleman a poet, too, Cytheris?"

"No; this is Hermogenes — he is as humorous as a poet, though; he is a musician," Cytheris said.

"Humorous" can refer to moods.

"A musician?" Chloe said. "Then he can sing."

"That he can excellently," Cytheris said. "Have you never heard him?"

"Oh, no," Chloe said. "Will he be persuaded to sing, do you think?"

"I don't know," Cytheris said.

She then said to Gallus, "Friend, Mistress Chloe would like to hear Hermogenes sing. Do you have any influence over him?"

Gallus answered, "No doubt his own humanity and courtesy will command him so far, to the satisfaction of so fair a beauty; but rather than fail, we'll all be suitors to him."

"I cannot sing," Hermogenes said.

"Please, Hermogenes," Gallus said.

"I cannot sing," Hermogenes said.

Gallus pointed to Chloe and said, "For honor of this gentlewoman, to whose house I know thou may be ever welcome."

"That he shall in truth, sir, if he can sing," Chloe said.

Ovid, Julia, Tibullus, and Plautia joined the group around Hermogenes.

"Who's that?" Ovid asked.

"This gentlewoman is wooing Hermogenes for a song," Gallus said.

Ovid said:

"A song? Come, he shall not deny her.

"Hermogenes?"

"I cannot sing," Hermogenes said.

Gallus said to the others, "No, the ladies must persuade him; he waits just to have their thanks acknowledged as a debt to his skill."

"That shall not be lacking," Julia said. "We ourself will be the first who shall promise to pay him more than thanks upon a favor so worthily granted."

She was using the majestic plural.

"Thank you, madam, but I will not sing," Hermogenes said.

Tibullus said, "Tut, the only way to win him is to abstain from entreating him."

Crispinus said quietly to Chloe, "Do you love singing, lady?"

"Oh, surpassingly," Chloe said.

"Entreat the ladies to entreat me to sing, then, I beseech you," Crispinus said.

Chloe pointed to Crispinus and said to Julia, "I beg Your Grace, entreat this gentleman to sing."

"That we will, Chloe," Julia said. "Can he sing excellently?"

Chloe answered, "I think so, madam, for he entreated me to entreat you to entreat him to sing."

Crispinus said quietly to Chloe, "Heaven and earth! Why would you tell her that?"

Julia said to Crispinus, "Good sir, let's entreat you to use your voice."

"Alas, madam, I cannot, in truth," Crispinus said.

"The gentleman is modest," Plautia said. "I guarantee you that he sings excellently."

"Hermogenes, clear your throat," Ovid said. "I see by the look of him that here's a gentleman who will worthily challenge you."

"Not I, sir. I'll challenge no man," Crispinus said.

"That's your modesty, sir," Tibullus said, "but we, out of an assurance of your excellency, challenge him on your behalf."

"I thank you, gentlemen," Crispinus said. "I'll do my best."

Hermogenes said to Crispinus, "Let that best be good, sir. It will be best for you to be good."

"Oh, this contention is excellent," Gallus said.

He then said to Crispinus, "What is it you will sing, sir?"

Crispinus replied, "'If I freely may discover,' etc. Sir, I'll sing that."

Ovid said to Hermogenes, "It's one of your own compositions, Hermogenes. He offers you advantage enough."

Crispinus said, "Nay, truly, gentlemen, I'll challenge no man — I can sing but one stanza of the ditty, and no more."

"All the better," Gallus said. "Hermogenes himself will be entreated to sing the other."

Crispinus sang:

"*If I freely may discover [reveal]*

"*What would please me in my lover,*

"*I would have her fair and witty,*

"*Savoring more of court than city;*

"*A little proud, but full of pity;*

"*Light and humorous [full of fancies] in her toying,*

"*Oft [Often] building hopes, and soon destroying,*

"*Long, but sweet, in the enjoying [in having sex];*

"*Neither too easy nor too hard:*

"*All extremes I would have barred.*"

Gallus said to Crispinus, "Believe me, sir, you sing most excellently."

"If there were a praise above excellence, the gentleman highly deserves it," Ovid said.

Hermogenes said to Crispinus, "Sir, all this does not yet make me envy you, for I know I sing better than you."

Tibullus said to all the others, "Listen to Hermogenes now."

Hermogenes sang:

"*She should be allowed her passions,*

"*So [So long as] they were [would be] but used as fashions:*

"*Sometimes froward [hard to please], and then frowning,*

"*Sometimes sickish, and then swowning [swooning],*

"*Every fit with change still crowning.*

"*[Crowning every fit with change always.]*

"*Purely jealous I would have her,*

"*Then only constant when I crave her;*

"*'Tis a virtue should not save her.*

"*Thus, nor her delicates [delights] would cloy me*

"*Neither her peevishness annoy me.*"

This was an anti-love song. The final five lines can be paraphrased like this:

"I would have her be completely jealous,

"But then when I desire her I would have her be completely chaste.

"Her virtue of chasteness would not save her from my dislike.

"Thus, her sexual delights would not cloy me,

"And neither would her peevishness annoy me."

Julia said, "Nay, Hermogenes, your merit has long since been both known and admired by us."

"You shall hear me sing another song," Hermogenes said. "Now will I begin."

Gallus motioned toward Albius and said, "We shall do this gentleman's banquet that waits for us, ladies, too much wrong."

To ignore the banquet would wrong it.

Julia said, "That is true; and well thought on, Cornelius Gallus."

The company began to move towards the dining chamber.

Hermogenes said, "Why, it is but a short air; it will be done quickly; please stay."

He said to the musicians in the gallery, "Strike, music!"

Ovid said, "No, good Hermogenes; we'll end this difference — this dispute about who is the better singer — inside."

Julia said to Ovid, "It is the common disease of all your musicians, that they know no mean to be entreated either to begin or end."

Musicians are difficult to convince to begin and difficult to convince to stop.

Albius said to the others, "Will it please you to lead the way, gentles?"

Because the gentles were of a higher social rank, they would lead the way to the banquet.

The gentles replied, "Thanks, good Albius."

Everybody except Albius and Crispinus exited.

Albius said to himself:

"Oh, what a charm — a chorus — of thanks was here put upon me! O Jove, what a setting forth of social status it is to a man to have many courtiers come to his house! Sweetly was it said by a good old housekeeper, 'I had rather lack meat — food — than lack guests' — especially if they are courtly guests."

Good guests are better than good food.

Albius continued:

"For never trust me if one of their good legs — that is, bows — made in a house is not worth all the good food and drink a man can make them. He who would have fine guests, let him have a fine wife; he who would have a fine wife, let him come to me."

"By your kind leave, Master Albius," Crispinus said.

Crispinus was interested in Albius' fine wife.

"What! You have not gone in to the banquet, Master Crispinus?" Albius said.

"Indeed, I have a project that draws me away from here," Crispinus said. "Please, sir, make an excuse for me to the ladies."

"Will you not stay and see the jewels, sir?" Albius asked. "I ask you, stay."

"Not for a million, sir, now," Crispinus said. "Let it suffice, I must relinquish; and so, in a word, please expiate this compliment."

By "relinquish," he meant "leave."

By "expiate," he meant "expedite."

By "compliment," he meant "excuse."

Albius said, "Mum."

"Mum" meant "Silent."

If Crispinus could misuse words, so could Albius.

Albius exited.

Alone, Crispinus said to himself, "I'll presently go and ingle some pawnbroker for a poet's gown and bespeak a garland; and then, jeweler, look to your best jewel, indeed."

By "ingle," he meant "wheedle."

Pawnbrokers dealt in second-hand goods.

Poets tend to be impoverished, and any good clothing they own must eventually end up in a pawnbroker's shop.

By "bespeak a garland," Crispinus meant that he was going to order a poet's wreath.

Albius' best jewel was his wife: Chloe.

Crispinus exited.

CHAPTER 3

— 3.1 —

Alone on Holy Street, aka *Via Sacra*, Horace, a fine poet, said to himself, "Hmm? Yes. I will begin an ode so; and it shall be to Maecenas."

Crispinus entered the scene and said, "By God's eyelid, yonder's Horace! They say he's an excellent poet; Maecenas loves him. I'll fall into his acquaintance if I can. I think he is composing as he goes in the street. Hmm? It is a good humor — poetic characteristic — if he is; I'll compose, too."

Horace recited to himself:

"*Swell me a bowl with lusty wine*

"*Till I may see the plump Lyaeus [the god Bacchus] swim*

"*Above the brim;*

"*I drink as I would write,*

"*In flowing measure filled with flame and sprightly spirit.*"

Crispinus said:

"Sweet Horace, may Minerva and the Muses stand auspicious to thy projects!"

Minerva is the goddess of wisdom, and the Muses are goddesses of the arts.

Crispinus continued:

"How do thou fare, sweet man? Frolicsome? Rich? Gallant? Huh?"

"Not greatly gallant, sir," Horace said. "Like my fortunes, I am well. I'm bold to take my leave, sir. You'd want nothing else with me, sir, would you?"

Horace wanted to leave Crispinus' presence.

Crispinus said, "Indeed, no, but I could wish thou did know us, Horace. We are a scholar, I assure thee."

"A scholar, sir?" Horace said. "I shall be covetous of your fair knowledge."

"Gramercy, good Horace," Crispinus said. "Thank you. We are newly turned poet, too, which is more; and a satirist, too, which is more than that. I write just in thy vein, I. I am for your odes or your sermons, or anything, indeed. We are a gentleman, besides: our name is Rufus Laberius Crispinus. We are a pretty Stoic, too."

Horace wrote books titled *Odes* and *Satires*. The *Satires* were sometimes called *Sermones*, which means *Conversations*.

"To the proportion — the length — of your beard, I think it, sir," Horace said.

Long beards are sometimes regarded as signs of wisdom. The actor playing Crispinus would have little or no beard, or a false beard.

Crispinus said, "By Phoebus, here's a most neat fine street, isn't it? I protest to thee I am enamored of this street, now, more than I am of half the streets of Rome, again; it is so polite and terse! There's the front of a building, now. I study architecture, too; if ever I should build, I'd have a house just of that prospective."

The word "terse" means "not using many words."

"Polite and terse" is a compliment when applied to people.

A prospective is a place that provides a good view. Or it may be simply the attractive front of a building.

Horace said to himself, "Doubtless this gallant's tongue has a good turn when he sleeps."

How about a good turn when the gallant is awake? Not so much.

Crispinus said, "I make verses when I come in such a street as this. Oh, the city ladies, they sit in every shop like the Muses — offering the Castalian dews and the Thespian liquors to as many as have just the sweet grace and audacity to sip of their lips."

The wives of tradesmen would sit in the windows of shops and encourage customers to shop there.

Castalia was a spring sacred to the Muses.

Thespis was the father of Greek tragedy. From his name we get the word "thespian" — actor.

Crispinus asked, "Did you ever hear any of my verses?"

Horace answered, "No, sir."

He said to himself, "But I am in some fear I must hear your verses now."

Crispinus said, "I'll tell thee some (if I can but recover them) that I composed just now about a hair dressing I saw a jeweler's wife wear, who indeed was a jewel herself. I prefer that kind of headdress, now."

He was talking about Chloe.

Crispinus then asked, "What's thy opinion, Horace?"

"With your silver bodkin, it does well, sir," Horace said.

A bodkin is a long pin used in hair dressings or as a cap decoration.

Horace was talking about Crispinus.

Crispinus said:

"I cannot tell why, but it stirs me more than all your court-curls or your spangles — sequins — or your tricks — knick-knacks. I don't like these high gable ends, these Tuscan tops, nor your coronets, nor your arches, nor your pyramids."

These were then-current styles in ladies' hairdressings.

Crispinus continued:

"Give me a fine, sweet — little delicate dressing, with a bodkin, as you say, and I don't give a mushroom for all your other ornatures — embellishments."

"Isn't it possible to make an escape from him?" Horace said to himself.

Crispinus was a bore.

"I have remitted my verses all this while," Crispinus said. "I think I have forgotten them."

"Remit" means "refrain from inflicting a punishment." Crispinus had forgotten his poems and so he could not inflict them on Horace.

Crispinus had only recently decided to be a poet. In fact, he had written his first poem a couple of minutes ago. No wonder Horace had not heard any of Crispinus' verses.

"Here's a person — me — who could wish you had, if not," Horace said to himself.

"I pray Jove that I can entreat them from my memory," Crispinus said.

"You put your memory to too much trouble, sir," Horace said.

"No, sweet Horace, we must not have thee think so," Crispinus said.

"I beg your pardon," Horace said.

He then said to himself, "Then they are my ears that must be tortured. Well, you must have patience, ears."

"Please, Horace, observe," Crispinus said.

By "observe," he meant "listen." Crispinus had remembered his poem.

Horace looked him over and said, "Yes, sir. Your satin sleeve begins to fret at the rug that is underneath it, I do observe; and your ample velvet bases are not without evident stains of a hot disposition naturally."

Crispinus' sleeve had two layers. The outer expensive satin layer was wearing away, revealing the rough "rug," a kind of cloth, underneath. And his middle-lower men's garment — velvet bases — showed sweat stains, or possibly, stains of sexual activity, revealing that he had a lustful temperament.

"Oh, I'll dye them into another color at my pleasure," Crispinus said. "How many yards of velvet do thou think they contain?"

Velvet was an expensive fabric. Clothing with lots of velvet would be expensive.

Horace said to himself, "By God's heart! I have put him now in a fresh way to vex me more."

He then said to Crispinus, "Indeed, sir, your mercer's book will tell you with more patience than I can."

He then said to himself, "For I am crossed, and your mercer's book is not crossed, I think."

A mercer is a dealer in fine fabrics such as velvet. Merchants gave credit to some customers. When a customer paid off the debt, the debt was crossed off in the tradesman's account book.

"By God's light, these verses have lost me again," Crispinus said. "I shall not invite them to my mind now."

"Rack not your thoughts, good sir," Horace said. "Rather defer it to a new time. I'll meet you at your lodging or wherever you please. Until then, Jove keep you, sir."

Horace started to leave.

"Nay, gentle Horace, stay," Crispinus said. "I have it now. I remember my poem now."

"Yes, sir," Horace said.

He then prayed silently, "Apollo, Hermes, Jupiter, look down upon me."

Crispinus recited his poem out loud:

"Rich was thy hap [fortune], sweet, dainty cap [a city fashion]

"There to be placed:

"Where thy smooth black, sleek white may smack [kiss loudly],

"And both be graced."

The woman's cap was lucky because it could kiss — touch — the woman's forehead.

Crispinus then said:

"'White' is there usurped" — he meant "substituted" — "for her brow: her forehead; and then 'sleek,' as the parallel to 'smooth' that went before. A kind of paranomasy or agnomination; do you conceive, sir?"

Paranomasy and agnomination are names for the same figure of speech, one that involves using a word to allude to a different word, or using the same word but with two different meanings (a pun).

"Excellent," Horace said. "Indeed, sir, I must be abrupt and leave you."

"Why, what haste do thou have?" Crispinus said. "Please, stay a little. Thou shall not go yet, by Phoebus Apollo."

"I shall not?" Horace said.

He then said to himself, "What remedy — plan — can I come up with to leave? Bah, how I sweat with suffering!"

Crispinus said, "And then —"

He was ready to recite another poem.

"Please, sir, give me leave to wipe my face a little," Horace said.

Of course, he would have liked to have leave — permission — to leave.

"Yes, do, good Horace," Crispinus said.

"Thank you, sir," Horace said.

He then said to himself:

"By God's death! I must beg his permission to piss, soon, or beg his permission to leave so that I may go away from here with half my teeth — before I am an old man. I am in some such fear.

"This tyranny is strange, to take my ears up by commission whether or not I am willing, and make them lay-stalls — repositories of worthless stuff — to his lewd solecisms and worded trash."

Solecisms are irregularities in language. One meaning of "lewd" is "unlettered."

Horace continued saying to himself:

"Happy are thou, bold Bolanus, now, I say, whose freedom and impatience of this fellow would long before this have called him 'fool,' and 'fool,' and 'rank and tedious fool,' and have slung jests as hard as stones until thou had pelted him out of the place, while my tame modesty suffers — allows — my wit to be made a solemn ass to bear his fopperies."

Bolanus, a friend to Cicero, had a hot temper and would not put up with someone such as Crispinus but would be intentionally rude to him and so get rid of him.

Crispinus said, "Horace, thou are miserably desirous to be gone, I see. But — please, let's prove — attempt — to enjoy thee awhile. Thou have no business, I assure myself. To where is thy journey directed, huh?"

"Sir, I am going to visit a friend who is sick," Horace said.

"A friend? Who's he? Do I know him?" Crispinus asked.

"No, sir, you do not know him," Horace said.

He then said to himself, "And your not knowing him is not the worse for him."

"What's his name? Where's he lodged?" Crispinus asked.

"Where I shall be fearful to draw you out of your way, sir: a great distance from here," Horace said. "Please, sir, let's part."

"Nay, but where is it?" Crispinus said. "I ask thee, tell me."

Horace answered, "On the far side of the Tiber River."

He pointed and said, "Yonder, by Caesar's gardens."

These were the gardens that Julius Caesar had left to the Roman people in his will.

"Oh, that's my course directly," Crispinus said. "I am ready to go with you. Come, go. Why do thou stand here?"

"Yes, sir," Horace said. "By the Virgin Mary, the plague is in that part of the city; I had almost forgotten to tell you, sir."

"Bah!" Crispinus said. "That doesn't matter; I fear no pestilence. I have not offended Phoebus."

Phoebus Apollo was the god of plague.

Horace said to himself, "I have offended Phoebus Apollo, it seems, or else this heavy scourge could never have alighted on me —"

"Come along," Crispinus said. "Let's go."

Horace pointed in a different direction from the one he had first pointed to, and he said, "I am to go down some half mile this way, sir, first, to speak with his physician; and from thence to his apothecary, where I shall stay during the mixing of many different drugs —"

"Why, it's all one," Crispinus said. "I have nothing to do, and I don't love to be idle; I'll bear thee company. What do thou call the apothecary?"

Horace said to himself, "Oh, I wish that I knew a name that would frighten him, now!"

He then said out loud, "Sir, his name is Rhadamanthus; Rhadamanthus, sir. There's one so called by the same name who is a just judge in hell and inflicts strange vengeance on all those who here on earth torment poor patient spirits."

Dante has no circle exclusively for boors in his *Inferno*. An oversight? Perhaps boors are punished where thieves are punished: Boors steal time.

"He dwells at the Three Furies, by Janus' temple?" Crispinus asked.

"Your apothecary does, sir," Horace said.

"By God's heart, I owe him money for sweetmeats, and he has brought a legal action to arrest me, I hear," Crispinus said, "but —"

Horace interrupted, "Sir, I have made a most solemn vow: I will never bail any man."

Horace would not pay Crispinus' debt to the apothecary.

"Well, then, I'll swear and speak fair words to him, if the worst should come," Crispinus said. "But his name is Minos, not Rhadamanthus, Horace."

"That may be, sir," Horace said. "I just guessed at his name by his sign. But your Minos is a judge, too, sir!"

Minos is another judge in the Underworld.

Crispinus said:

"I protest to thee, Horace, do but taste me — try me out — once. If I know myself and my own virtues truly, thou will not make that esteem of Varius, or Virgil, or Tibullus, or any of them indeed, as now in thy ignorance thou do, which I am content to forgive."

In other words: If you, Horace, get to know me better, you will not hold in such high esteem Varius, or Virgil, or Tibullus, or your other poet-friends.

Lucius Varius Rufus, a poet-friend of Virgil, the author of the *Aeneid*, had introduced Horace to Maecenas.

Crispinus continued:

"I would like to see which of these could pen more verses in a day, or with more facility, than I; or see who could court his mistress, kiss her hand, make better sport with her fan or her dog —"

"I cannot bail you yet — for all that — sir," Horace interrupted.

Crispinus continued:

"— or who could move his body more gracefully, or dance better. You should see me dance, if we were not in the street —"

"Nor yet," Horace said.

He still would not pay Crispinus' debt to the apothecary.

Crispinus said, "Why, I have been a reveler, and at my cloth of silver suit and my long stocking in my time, and will be again —"

"My cloth of silver suit and my long stocking" were party clothes. "Cloth of silver" was expensive fabric sewn with silver thread. Dancers wore long stockings.

Horace said, "If you may be trusted, sir."

Crispinus will dance again if mercers will trust him and give him credit to buy fancy cloth and clothing.

"And then for my singing," Crispinus said, "Hermogenes himself envies me. He is the only master of music that you have in Rome."

"Is your mother living, sir?" Horace asked.

"Au!" Crispinus said. "Convert thy thoughts to something else, please."

"Au" is an expression of woe.

"You have much of the mother in you, sir," Horace said. "Your father is dead?"

"The mother" means "hysteria." But Horace may have meant that Crispinus was effeminate.

"Aye, I thank Jove, and my grandfather, too, and all my kinsfolks, and they are well composed in their urns," Crispinus said.

"Well composed" means "at peace."

"Well 'composed" means "well decomposed."

Horace said to himself, "The more their happiness, who rest in peace, free from the abundant torture of thy tongue. I wish that I were with them, too."

"What's that, Horace?" Crispinus asked.

Horace said, "I now remember, sir, a sad fate a cunning woman, a fortune teller, one Sabella, sung when in her urn she cast — forecast by casting lots — my destiny, when I was just a child."

"What sad fate was it, please?" Crispinus asked.

Horace answered:

"She told me I should surely never perish by famine, poison, or the enemy's sword. The hectic fever, cough, or pleurisy should never hurt me, nor the movement-retarding and late-in-life-coming gout. But in my time I should be once surprised and taken unawares by a strong, tedious talker, who should vex me and almost bring me to consumption.

"Therefore, she warned me if I were wise to shun all such long-winded monsters as my bane. For if I could but escape that one discourser, I might, no doubt, prove to become an old, aged man."

Ready to leave, he said, "By your leave, sir?"

Crispinus said:

"Tut, tut, abandon this idle humor; it is nothing but melancholy.

"Before Jove, now that I think of it, I am to appear in court here to answer to one who has a lawsuit against me.

"Sweet Horace, go with me. This is my hour; if I neglect it, the law will proceed against me. Thou are familiar with these things. Please, if thou respect me, go with me."

Horace said:

"Now let me die, sir, if I know the laws or have the power to stand still half so long in the laws' loud courts, while a case is argued.

"Besides, you know, sir, where I am to go, and the necessity —"

Crispinus interrupted, "That is true —"

Horace said to himself, "I hope that the hour of my release has come! He will upon this consideration discharge me, surely."

"Indeed, I am doubtful what I may best do: whether to leave thee, or my affairs, Horace," Crispinus said.

"O Jupiter!" Horace said. "Leave me, sir; leave me, by any means. I beseech you, leave me, sir."

"No, in faith, I'll risk ignoring my affairs for now," Crispinus said. "Thou shall see I love and respect thee. Come, Horace."

"Nay, then, I am desperate and out of hope," Horace said. "I follow you, sir. It is hard contending with a man who overcomes resistance in this way."

"And how deals Maecenas with thee?" Crispinus asked.

"Liberally, huh? Is he open-handed? Bountiful?"

Maecenas was a patron to Roman poets such as Horace.

"He's still himself, sir," Horace answered.

Crispinus said:

"Truly, Horace, thou are exceedingly happy and fortunate in thy friends and acquaintances: They are all the most choice spirits and of the first rank of Romans.

"I don't know any poet, I declare, who has used his good fortune more prosperously than thou have. If thou would make me known to Maecenas, I should second thy well-deserved good fortune well. Thou should find a good, sure assistant of me: one who would speak all good of thee in thy absence and be content with the place just under yours, not envying thy reputation with thy patron. Let me not live if I don't think thou and I, in a small time, should lift them all out of favor, both Virgil, Varius, and the best of them, and enjoy him wholly to ourselves."

Crispinus wanted to bring Horace's friends — Virgil, Varius, and the best of the other poets — out of favor with Maecenas.

Horace said to himself, "Gods, you do know it, I can hold myself back no longer. This breeze — this horsefly — has pricked my patience."

He said to Crispinus, "Sir, Your Silkness clearly mistakes Maecenas and his house, to think there breathes a spirit beneath his roof subject to those poor affections and emotions of undermining envy and detraction — moods proper only to base, groveling minds."

Such as the mind of Crispinus.

Horace continued:

"There is no place in Rome, I dare affirm, that is purer or freer from such low, common evils than Maecenas' house. In the house of Maecenas, no man is grieved that this man is thought richer or this other man is thought more learned. Each man has his place, and to each man's merit Maecenas gives his reward of grace, which with a mutual love they all embrace."

"You report a wonder!" Crispinus said. "It is scarcely credible, this."

"I am no torturer to force you to believe it, but it is so," Horace said.

"Why, this inflames me with a more ardent desire to be his than before," Crispinus said. "But I fear I shall find the entrance to his familiarity — to himself and to his intimate circle — somewhat more than difficult, Horace."

"Tut, you'll conquer him as you have conquered me," Horace said. "There's no standing against and resisting you, sir; I see that. Either your importunity or the intimation of your good qualities, or —"

Crispinus was unwilling to rely on his "good" qualities, so he said:

"Nay, I'll bribe his porter and the servants of his chamber, and make his doors open to me that way first; and then I'll observe my times to see the best time to approach him.

"If he should extrude and expel me from his house today, shall I therefore desist, or abandon my suit tomorrow? No. I'll attend him, follow him, meet him in the street, the highways, run by his coach, never leave him.

"What! Man has nothing given to him in this life without much labor."

Horace said, under his breath:

"And impudence.

"Archer of heaven, Phoebus, take thy bow and with a full-drawn arrow-shaft nail to the earth this Python, so that I may yet run away from here and live."

Phoebus Apollo killed a python that guarded Delphi. Afterward, Delphi became a site sacred to Apollo.

Horace continued saying to himself:

"Or, brawny Hercules, come down and — although thou make it thy thirteenth labor — rescue me from this Hydra of discourse here."

Hercules' second labor of twelve was killing the Lernaean Hydra. In accomplishing this labor, Hercules had the help of a nephew named Iolaus. The Hydra of Lerna had nine heads, the middle of which was immortal. Hercules and Iolaus traveled to Lerna and found the Hydra's lair. Hercules forced the Hydra to leave its lair by shooting flaming arrows into the lair. Hercules fought the Hydra, but he discovered that each time a mortal head was cut off, two more heads grew in its place. Hera gave Hercules even more trouble by sending an enormous crab to fight him, but Hercules crushed the crab. Hercules then got help from Iolaus. Each time Hercules cut off one of the Hydra's mortal heads, Iolaus cauterized it with a torch, thus preventing more heads from growing. Hercules then cut off the immortal head and placed it under a boulder. The blood of the Hydra was poisonous, and before leaving, Hercules dipped the heads of his arrows into the Hydra's blood.

Fuscus Aristius, a scholar and writer, and one of Horace's friends, entered the scene.

"Horace, we are well met," Aristius said.

Horace said quietly to Aristius, "Oh, welcome, my reliever! Aristius, as thou love and respect me, ransom me."

"What ails thou, man?" Aristius asked.

Horace said quietly:

"By God's death, I am seized on here by a land-remora."

A remora was a kind of sucking fish that was thought to be able to attach itself to a ship and retard its progress.

He continued quietly:

"I cannot stir, cannot move, except as he please."

"Will thou go, Horace?" Crispinus asked.

Horace said quietly:

"By God's heart! He cleaves to me like Alcides' shirt, tearing my flesh and sinews."

"Alcides" means "Hercules, aka Heracles."

A Centaur named Nessus once tried to rape Deianira, Hercules' wife. Hercules and Deianeira had to cross a river. Nessus offered to carry Deianeira across the river, but then he attempted to rape her. Hercules shot him with an arrow whose head had been dipped into the poisonous blood of the Hydra. Before Nessus died, he told Deianeira that his blood had a magical quality; it was a love potion. He said that if Deianeira were to ever think that Hercules was in love with someone else, she could make him love her again by smearing Nessus' blood on the inside of a robe and then giving it to Hercules to wear. Deianeira believed him, but it was a trick. She thought that Hercules was falling in love with someone else, so she did what Nessus had told her to do, but Hercules' arrow had poisoned the blood of the Centaur. When Hercules put on the robe, Nessus' blood, which was infected by the poisonous blood of the Hydra, burned Hercules like acid, as Nessus had known it would. In agony, Hercules climbed on a funeral pyre, lit it, and burned himself to death. Once dead, he became a god and lived on Mount Olympus.

Horace continued quietly:

"Oh, I have been vexed and tortured with him beyond forty fevers.

"For Jove's sake, find some means to take me from him!"

Aristius said loudly, "Yes, I will, but I'll go first and tell Maecenas."

Crispinus said to Horace, "Come, shall we go?"

Aristius said loudly, "The jest will make his eyes run with tears of laughter, indeed."

He started to leave.

"Nay, Aristius?" Horace said.

"Farewell, Horace," Aristius said, leaving.

"By God's death! Will he leave me?" Horace said.

He called after him, "Fuscus Aristius, do you hear me? Gods of Rome!"

Aristius returned, and Horace said, "You said you had something to say to me in private."

"Aye, but I see that you are now employed with that gentleman," Aristius said. "It would be an offence to trouble you. I'll take some better opportunity; farewell."

He exited.

Horace said, "Mischief and torment! O my soul and heart, how you are cramped with anguish! Death itself brings not the like convulsions. O this day! That ever I should view the day's tedious face —"

"Horace, what passion, what humor is this?" Crispinus asked.

"Away, good monster," Horace said. "Don't afflict me."

He said to himself, "Crispinus? A friend, and mock me thus! Never was a man so left under the axe."

Was the axe used in sacrifice or in execution?

He then asked, "What is this now?"

Minos and two Lictors entered the scene. Lictors had the power to arrest people. Minos was the apothecary to whom Crispinus owed money.

A short distance from Crispinus, Minos pointed him out to the Lictors and said, "That's he in the embroidered hat there, with the ash-colored feather: His name is Laberius Crispinus."

The two Lictors came forward, and the First Lictor said, "Laberius Crispinus, I arrest you in the Emperor's name."

"Me, sir?" Crispinus asked. "Do you arrest me?"

"Aye, sir, at the suit of Master Minos the apothecary," the First Lictor answered.

Horace said to himself, "Thanks, great Apollo! I will not let slip — will not overlook — thy favor offered me in my escape, for my fortunes."

He definitely did not want to let slip his chance to escape.

Unobserved by Crispinus, Horace exited.

"Master Minos? I know no Master Minos," Crispinus said.

He looked around and said, "Where's Horace? Horace? Horace?"

Coming forward, Minos asked, "Sir, don't you know me?"

Seeing him, Crispinus said, "Oh, yes, I know you, Master Minos, I beg your pardon. But Horace? God's me, has he gone?"

"Aye, and so would you, too, if you knew how," Minos said.

He then said to the First Lictor, "Officer, look to him."

The Lictors approached Crispinus to arrest him and take him away.

"Listen, Master Minos," Crispinus said. "Please let us be treated like a man of our own fashion. By Janus and Jupiter, I meant to have paid you next week every drachma I owe you. Don't seek to eclipse and darken my reputation thus vulgarly and publicly."

"Sir, your oaths cannot serve you," Minos said. "You know I have forborne you a long time."

He had waited a long time for the debt to be repaid, and the debt had not been repaid.

"I am conscious of it, sir," Crispinus said.

The Lictors grabbed him and began to haul him away.

Crispinus said, "Nay, I beg you, gentlemen, do not exhale me thus; remember my debt is only for sweetmeats —"

By "exhale me," he meant "haul me away."

"Sweet meat must have sour sauce, sir," the First Lictor said. "Come along."

The Lictors began to drag Crispinus away.

"Sweet Master Minos!" Crispinus said. "I am forfeited to eternal disgrace if you do not commiserate."

He wanted Minos to take pity on him.

He said to the First Lictor, "Good officer, be not so officious — so zealous in your work."

Tucca entered the scene with two of his Pyrgi.

Tucca said to the Lictors, "Why, how are you now, my good pair of bloodhounds? Whither do you drag the gentleman? You mongrels, you curs, you bandogs, we are Captain Tucca who is talking to you, you inhumane — inhuman and uncivilized — pilchers."

Bandogs are attack dogs that are kept chained up.

A pilcher is a worthless person.

Minos said to Tucca, "Sir, he is their prisoner."

"Their pestilence!" Tucca said. "Who are you, sir?"

"A citizen of Rome, sir," Minos said.

"Then you are not far distant from a fool, sir," Tucca said.

"I am an apothecary, sir," Minos said.

"I knew thou weren't a physician," Tucca said. "I can tell by the smell."

He sniffed Minos and then said, "Bah! Get out of my nostrils! Thou stink of lotium and the syringe. Away, quacksalver!"

"Lotium" is stale urine, used as a hair dressing.

A quacksalver is a quack: a bad physician.

Tucca said to the first Pyrgus, "Follower, my sword!"

The first Pyrgus handed him his sword and said, "Here, noble leader."

He then said to himself, "You'll do no harm with it, I'll trust you."

Tucca said to the First Lictor:

"Do you hear, you, goodman slave? Hook, ram, rogue, catchpole!"

Arresting officers sometimes used a staff with a hook. Battering-rams were used to batter down doors. Catchpoles were officers who arrested debtors.

Tucca continued:

"Let loose the gent'man, or by my velvet arms —"

The First Lictor kicked Tucca's heels and knocked him to the ground.

Catching Tucca's sword, the First Lictor said, "What will you do, sir?"

"Kiss thy hand, my honorable active varlet, and embrace thee, like this," Tucca said, attempting to perform the actions.

The First Pyrgus said to himself, "Oh, patient metamorphosis!"

Tucca had quickly metamorphosed into a patient man.

Tucca said to the First Lictor, "My sword, my tall — brave and valiant — rascal."

"Nay, not so fast, sir," the First Lictor said. "Some of us are wiser than some others."

"What! And a wit, too!" Tucca said. "By Pluto, thou must be cherished, slave."

He gave the First Lictor money and said, "Here's three drachmas for thee; hold."

He meant for the Lictor to hold off from arresting this man.

The First Pyrgus said to himself, "There's half his lendings gone."

Tucca's "lendings" consisted of the six drachmas he had "borrowed" — that is, conned — from Ovid Senior.

Tucca said to the First Lictor, "Give me the sword."

"No, sir, your first word shall stand," the First Lictor said. "I'll hold all."

He would hold on to the sword and the money.

Tucca started to argue, "Nay, but, rogue —"

The First Lictor said, "You would make a forcible rescue of our prisoner, sir, would you?"

"I, a rescue?" Tucca said. "Go away, inhuman varlet! Come, come, I never relish above one jest at most; do not disgust me with your jests, sirrah, do not. Rogue, I tell thee, rogue, do not."

"What, sir? 'Rogue'?" the First Lictor said.

"Aye," Tucca said. "Why, thou are not angry, rascal? Are thou angry?"

"I cannot tell, sir," the First Lictor said. "I am little better than angry at these terms you are calling me."

Tucca said:

"Ha! Gods and fiends! Why, do thou hear? Rogue, thou, give me thy hand. I say unto thee, give me thy hand, rogue."

The First Lictor did not shake hands with him.

Tucca continued:

"What? Don't thou know me? Not me, rogue? Not Captain Tucca, rogue?"

Minos said to the First Lictor, "Come, please surrender the gentleman's sword to him, officer; we'll have no fighting here."

Tucca asked Minos, "What's thy name?"

"Minos, if it pleases you."

"Minos?" Tucca said. "Come here, Minos; thou are a wise fellow, it seems. Let me talk with thee."

Crispinus said, "Was ever any wretch as wretched as unfortunate I?"

Tucca and Minos talked together quietly.

Tucca flattered Minos, "Thou are one of the Centumviri, old boy, aren't thou?"

The Centumviri were a group of Romans who could be selected to serve as jurors in a civil court. The position was prestigious.

"No, indeed, Master Captain," Minos said.

"Come, thou shall be, then," Tucca said. "I'll have thee made one, Minos. Take my sword from those rascals, do thou see? Go, do it; I cannot attempt the deed with patience."

Tucca then said out loud, "What does this gent'man owe thee, little Minos?"

"Fourscore sesterces, sir," Minos answered.

Tucca said, "What? No more? Come, thou shall release him, Minos. Tell you what, I'll be his bail and put up security for his repayment of the debt; thou shall take my word, old boy, and cashier — dismiss — these Furies. Thou shall do it, I say, thou shall, little Minos, thou shall."

Literally, Furies are female avenging spirits from hell. Figuratively, they are the two Lictors.

"Yes; and as I am a gentleman and a reveler, I'll make a piece of poetry, and absolve — pay back — all within these five days," Crispinus said.

He was planning to write a poem for which Maecenas, patron of poets, would reward him with money.

Tucca said to Crispinus, "Come, Minos is not to learn — he already knows — how to treat a gent'man of quality, I know."

He then said to Minos, "Give me my sword. If he — Crispinus — does not repay thee, I will and I must, old boy. Thou shall be my apothecary, too. Have thou good eringoes, Minos?"

Eringoes are a kind of sweetmeat: candied sea holly root.

"The best in Rome, sir," Minos said.

"Go to, then," Tucca said.

"Go to" is commonly used in the phrase "Go to hell," but Tucca wanted to go to Minos' shop.

He said to his two Pyrgi, "Vermin, know the house."

In other words: Case Minos' shop for things that Tucca can con out of Minos.

"I promise you we will, Colonel," the First Pyrgus said.

Indicating Crispinus, Tucca said to Minos, "What about this gent'man, Minos?"

"I'll take your word, Captain," Minos said.

He would take Tucca's word that he would repay Crispinus' debt if Crispinus did not.

"Thou have it," Tucca said. "My sword —"

A military man needed a sword. It was a disgrace for him to be without one.

"Yes, sir," Minos replied.

He then said to Crispinus, "But you must discharge the arrest, Master Crispinus. You must pay the Lictors for their service."

In this society, police officers — Lictors — were paid to make an arrest.

"What, Minos!" Tucca said. "Look in the gent'man's face and just read his silence."

In other words: He is silent and distressed because he has no money.

Tucca then said, "Pay the Lictors, pay them; releasing a gent'man is the honorable thing to do, Minos."

Minos paid the Lictors, who released Crispinus.

Ignoring Minos, who was of a lower social class than he, Crispinus said to Tucca, "By Jove, sweet Captain, you do most infinitely endear and oblige me to you."

"Tut, I cannot compliment, by Mars; but may Jupiter love me as I love good words and good clothes, and there's an end to this," Tucca said. "Thou shall give my boy that girdle and hangers when thou have worn them a little more —"

Not being a true military man, Tucca could not compliment by Mars, god of war. "To compliment" means "to use ceremonious language."

A girdle is a belt. This belt had hangers: loops that could be used to carry weapons.

"O Jupiter!" Crispinus said. "Captain, he shall have them now, immediately."

He said to the First Pyrgus, "May it please you to be acceptive, young gentleman."

"Yes, sir, fear not," the First Pyrgus said. "I shall accept."

He then said to himself, "I have a pretty, foolish humor of taking, aka stealing, if you — Crispinus — knew all."

Tucca said to the First Pyrgus, "Not now. You shall not take, boy."

"By my truth and earnest, but he shall, Captain, by your leave," Crispinus said.

Tucca said to the First Pyrgus, "Well, if he swear by his truth and earnest, take it, boy. Do not make a gent'man forsworn."

Crispinus took off and gave his belt and hangers to the First Pyrgus while Tucca talked to the Lictors.

The First Lictor gave Tucca the sword he had confiscated and said, "Well, sir, there is your sword; but thank Master Minos. You would not have carried it — the sword and the situation — off as you do now, otherwise."

The Lictors started to leave.

Tucca said, "Minos is just, and you are knaves, and —"

The First Lictor turned back and said, "What did you say, sir?"

Tucca said:

"Pass on, my good scoundrel, pass on. I honor thee."

The Lictors started to leave.

Tucca added:

"But except that I hate to have action with such base rogues as these, you should have seen me unrip their noses now, and have sent them to the closest barber's for stitching; for, do you see —"

At this time, barbers also served as doctors.

The Lictors turned back.

Tucca hastily said:

"I am a man of humor, and I do love the varlets, the honest varlets; they have intelligence and valor, and are indeed good, profitable and useful —"

The Lictors exited.

Tucca concluded:

"— arrant rogues as any who live in an empire."

Tucca then said quietly to Crispinus, "Listen, poetaster. Second me. Back me up."

He said loudly, "Stand by me, Minos. Get close to me."

He said to Crispinus and Minos, "Gather closer yet. Good."

He said, "Sir," and then whispered to Crispinus, "thou shall have a quarter share; be resolute."

Tucca wanted to con Minos, and he wanted Crispinus to help in the con. If Crispinus helped, he would get part of what was conned from Minos.

Tucca then said loudly to Crispinus, "You shall, at my request, take Minos by the hand here, little Minos. I will have it so: all friends, and a toast to good health. Be not inexorable."

He then said to Minos:

"And thou shall impart — provide — the wine, old boy; thou shall do it, little Minos, thou shall; make us pay for it in our bill for medicine.

"What! We must live and honor the gods sometimes: Now Bacchus, now Comus, now Priapus — every god a little."

Bacchus is the god of drinking, Comus is the god of partying, and Priapus is the god of sex.

Histrio, an actor, entered the scene.

Tucca said:

"Who's he who stalks by there?

"Boy, Pyrgus, you were best to let him pass, sirrah. Do, ferret, let him pass, do."

"He is an actor, sir," the First Pyrgus said.

Learning that the man was only an actor, Tucca said:

"An actor? Call him; call the lousy slave hither.

"What! Will he sail by and not once strike or vail to a man-of-war, huh?"

A lesser ship would lower its flag as a sign of respect to a war ship. Tucca wanted the actor to take off his hat to honor him.

Tucca called to Histrio, "Do you hear me? You, actor, rogue, stalker! Come back here! No respect to men of worship, you slave?"

Histrio turned back and approached Tucca.

Tucca said:

"What! You are proud, you rascal? Are you proud, huh? You grow rich, do you? And purchase possessions, you twopenny tearmouth?"

Twopenny tearmouths were actors who ranted and raved and pleased audience members in the two-penny seats.

Tucca continued:

"You have Fortune and the good year on your side, you stinkard? Have you? Have you?"

"What the goodyear!" meant "What the Dickens!" The phrase "the goodyear" was used negatively in imprecations.

"Nay, sweet Captain, be confined to some reason," Histrio said. "I protest — declare — I didn't see you, sir."

Tucca replied:

"You did not? Where was your sight, Oedipus?"

Oedipus blinded himself in Sophocles' tragedy *Oedipus Rex*.

Tucca continued:

"You sleepwalk with hare's eyes, do you?"

Hares were believed to sleep with their eyes open.

Tucca continued:

"I'll have them glazed, rogue; if you say the word, they shall be glazed for you."

"Glazed" means 1) wear eyeglasses, or 2) beat you so that your eyes are glazed with tears.

Tucca continued:

"Come, we must have you turn fiddler again, slave, get a bass — or base — violin at your back and march in a tawny coat with one sleeve — a minstrel's costume with only one sleeve due to poverty — to Green Goose Fair."

Many actors were also musicians.

Tucca continued:

"— and then you'll know us; you'll see us then. You will, you gulch — you drunk and glutton — you will."

Mimicking a strolling musician, Tucca said, "Then you'll say, 'Will it please Your Worship to have any music, Captain?'"

Laughing, Histrio said, "Nay, good Captain."

Tucca said:

"What! Do you laugh, Owlglass? Do you laugh, jester?"

Owlglass was the hero of a German jest book: *Til Eulenspiegel*. The German name *Eulenspiegel* means "Owl Mirror." A glass is a mirror.

Tucca continued:

"By God's death, you perstemptuous varlet, I am none of your fellows; I have commanded a hundred and fifty such rogues, I!"

"Perstemptuous" is Tucca-speak for "presumptuous." And, possibly, it is a portmanteau word that includes the meanings of "contemptuous" and "preposterous."

The First Pyrgus said to himself, "Aye, and most of that hundred and fifty have been leaders of a legion."

That is, a legion of lice.

"A hundred and fifty" is a unit of infantry.

"If I have exhibited — presented and manifested — wrong, I'll tender satisfaction, Captain," Histrio said.

"Say thou so, honest vermin?" Tucca said. "Give me thy hand; thou shall make us a supper one of these nights."

"Make us a supper" means "pay for a meal for us at a tavern."

"When you please, by Jove, Captain, most willingly," Histrio said.

Pleased by the answer, Tucca said:

"Do thou swear? Tomorrow, then. Say and hold, slave: Perform what you say you will perform. Some of you actors are honest gent'manlike scoundrels and suspected to have some wit as well as your poets, both at drinking and breaking of jests, and are companions for gallants. A man may skelder — con — ye now and then of half a dozen shillings or so."

He pointed at Crispinus and asked:

"Don't thou know that Pantolabus there?"

Pantolabus is a bankrupt parasite who lives at others' expense in William Fullonius' *Acolastus*, a Latin school play of the sixteenth century. John Palsgrave translated the play into English.

"No, I assure you, Captain," Histrio said.

Tucca said:

"Go and be acquainted with him, then. He is a gent'man, a parcel-poet, aka part-poet, you slave. His father was a man of worship, I tell thee. Go! He pens high, lofty, in a new stalking strain, bigger than half the rhymers in the town, again; he was born to fill thy mouth, Minotaurus, he was."

A Minotaurus is the Minotaur, a part-man, part-bull monster that bellows like a bull.

According to Tucca, Crispinus was born to fill Histrio's mouth with words to speak on the stage.

Tucca continued:

"He will teach thee, rascal, to tear and rand — rend and rant. Go to him; cherish his muse, go! Thou have forty, forty — shillings, I mean, stinkard. Give them to him in earnest — as an advance — do. He shall write for thee, slave."

Whenever Tucca mentioned a number, he had to think about what was the greatest amount of money he could get from a person. Should he ask for shillings, or for drachmas, or for sesterces?

Tucca continued:

"If he pen for thee once, thou shall not need to travel with thy pumps full of gravel any more after a blind jade — broken-down horse — pulling a cart with a hamper containing costumes, and stalk upon boards and barrel heads to the accompaniment of an old, cracked trumpet —"

Sometimes, barrels held up the boards forming the stage.

According to Tucca, if Crispinus writes a play for Histrio, Histrio won't need to be an impoverished actor any longer.

Apparently, either Histrio will become a rich actor or will be forced to find work different from acting.

"In truth, I think I have not so much money about me, Captain," Histrio said.

Tucca said:

"It doesn't matter; give him what thou have, Stifftoe."

Tragic actors wore stiff leather boots called buskins.

Tucca continued:

"I'll give my word for the rest. Though it lack a shilling or two, it skills not — it doesn't matter. Go, thou are an honest shifter; I'll have the statute repealed for thee."

An honest shifter is an honest haggler.

By statute, actors could be charged with being rogues or vagabonds unless their acting troupe had a high-ranking member of society as its patron.

Histrio went aside to take out his money from his purse so he could pay a down payment for Crispinus to write a play.

Tucca said, "Minos, I must tell thee, Minos" — he pointed to Crispinus — "thou have dejected yonder gent'man's spirit exceedingly by having him arrested. Do thou observe? Do thou note, little Minos?"

"Yes, sir," Minos said.

"Go to work, then," Tucca said. "Raise, recover his spirits, do. Don't allow him to droop in the sight of an actor, a rogue, a stager. Put twenty into his hand, twenty — sesterces, I mean, and let nobody see. Go, do it, the work shall commend itself: It is a good deed. Be Minos, a just person; I'll pay back the money."

"Yes, truly, Captain," Minos said.

He approached Crispinus.

The Second Pyrgus said to the First Pyrgus, "Don't we serve a notable sharker and con man?"

While Tucca and Histrio talked, Minos gave money to Crispinus.

Tucca said to Histrio, "And what new matters have you now afoot, sirrah, huh? I would eagerly come with my cockatrice" — a cockatrice is a prostitute — "one day and see a play, if I knew when there were a good bawdy one; but they say you have nothing but humors, revels, and satires that gird — sneer — and fart at the time, you slave."

Histrio said:

"No, I assure you, Captain, not we. Those plays are on the other side of the Tiber River."

Actually, the Thames River. Despite the play's setting of Rome, Ben Jonson's play is about London and Englishmen. No doubt Ben Jonson's satires were playing on the other side of the river.

Histrio continued:

"We have as much ribaldry in our plays as can be, as you would wish, Captain. All the sinners in the suburbs come and applaud our action daily."

Lots of people in the suburbs liked to see a play with the accompaniment of a prostitute.

Tucca said:

"I hear you'll bring me on the stage there: You'll play me, they say. I shall be presented by a set of copper-laced scoundrels of you."

Tucca thought he would be satirized in a play in which the actor portraying him would be wearing copper lace instead of expensive gold lace.

Tucca continued:

"By the life of Pluto, if you stage me, stinkard, your mansions shall sweat for it, your tabernacles [tents and pavilions], varlets, your Globes and your triumphs!"

If Tucca finds out that he has been satirized on stage, his anger will be so great that the buildings — such as the Globe Theatre — the plays are staged in will feel his wrath.

Histrio replied, "Not we, by Phoebus, Captain. Do not do us imputation without desert — don't criticize us unless we deserve it."

Tucca said, "I would not, my good twopenny rascal."

Would not do what?

Would not "do us imputation without desert"?

Would not "not do us imputation without desert"?

Tucca continued:

"Reach me thy neuf."

"Neuf" is Tucca-speak for "nieve," aka fist, aka hand.

They shook hands.

Tucca continued:

"Do thou hear me? What will thou give me a week for my brace of beagles here, my little point-trussers?"

Points are laces that tie men's hose (tights) to their doublets (jackets).

Tucca wanted to hire out his two Pyrgi as boy-actors.

Tucca continued:

"You shall have them act among ye."

"Ye" is the plural of "you."

Tucca said to the First Pyrgus, "Sirrah, you, pronounce —"

He then said to Histrio, "Thou shall hear him speak in King Darius' doleful strain."

The First Pyrgus recited:

"O doleful days! O direful deadly dump!

"O wicked world! and worldly wickedness!

"How can I hold [back] my fist from crying 'thump'

"In rue of this right rascal wretchedness!"

Tucca then said to the First Pyrgus, "In an amorous vein — manner — now, sirrah."

He then said to the others, "Peace. Quiet."

The First Pyrgus recited:

"*Oh, she is wilder and more hard withal*

"*Than beast or bird, or tree or stony wall.*

"*Yet might she love me to uprear her state;*

"*Aye, but perhaps she hopes some nobler mate.*

"*Yet might she love me to content her sire;*

"*Aye, but her reason masters her desire.*

"*Yet might she love me as her beauty's thrall;*

"*Aye, but I fear she cannot love at all.*"

Tucca said to the Second Pyrgus, "Now the horrible fierce soldier: you, sirrah."

The Second Pyrgus recited:

"*What? Will I brave [defy] thee? Aye, and beard thee [pull thy beard], too!*

"*A Roman spirit scorns to bear a brain*

"*So full of base pusillanimity.*"

"Excellent!" Histrio said.

Tucca said to Histrio, "Nay, thou shall see that which shall ravish — enchant — thee soon; prick up thine ears, stinkard."

He then said to his two Pyrgi, "The ghost, boys."

The First Pyrgus recited, "*Vindicta!*"

The Second Pyrgus recited, *Timoria!*"

The First Pyrgus recited, "*Vindicta!*"

The Second Pyrgus recited, "*Timoria!*"

The First Pyrgus recited, "*Veni!*"

The Second Pyrgus recited, "*Veni!*"

"*Timoria!*" means "Retribution!"

"*Vindicta!*" means "Revenge!"

"*Veni!*" means "I come!"

Tucca said to the Second Pyrgus, "Now thunder, sirrah: you, the rumbling actor."

Drums could be used to simulate thunder.

The Second Pyrgus said, "Aye, but somebody must cry 'murder!' then, in a small voice."

A small voice is a female's high voice.

"Your fellow sharer there shall do it," Tucca said.

The two sharers have shares in the profits of Tucca's cons.

Tucca said to the First Pyrgus, "Cry, sirrah, cry."

The Second Pyrgus beat a drum roll.

In a high voice, the Second Pyrgus cried, "*Murder! Murder!*"

The Second Pyrgus cried, "*Who calls out 'murder'?*"

He then said to the First Pyrgus, "*Lady, was it you?*"

"Oh, admirably good, I declare," Histrio said.

Tucca said to the Second Pyrgus, "Sirrah boy, brace your drum a little straiter — stretch the drumskin tighter — and do the other fellow there, he in the — what do thou call him?"

He said to the First Pyrgus, "And '*yet stay*,' too."

In Thomas Kidd's *The Spanish Tragedy* is a conversation between the villain Lorenzo and a servant. Tucca was trying to remember some of the character's dialogue since he couldn't remember the character's name.

The Second Pyrgus beat another drum roll.

He recited:

"*Nay, an [if] thou dalliest, then I am thy foe,*

"*And fear shall force what friendship cannot win.*

"*Thy death shall bury what thy life conceals:*

"*Villain! Thou diest for more respecting her —*"

The First Pyrgus recited, "*Oh, stay, my lord!*"

The Second Pyrgus continued reciting:

"*— than me.*

"*Yet speak the truth, and I will guerdon [reward] thee;*

"*But if thou dally once again, thou diest.*"

"Enough of this, boy," Tucca said.

The Second Pyrgus continued reciting:

"*Why then, lament therefore! Damned be thy guts*

"*Unto King Pluto's hell and princely Erebus!*

"*For sparrows must have food.*"

Histrio said, "Please, sweet Captain, let one of them do a little of a lady."

"Oh, he will make thee eternally enamored of him there," Tucca said.

He said to the First Pyrgus, "Do, sirrah, do; it will allay your fellow's fury a little."

The First Pyrgus said in a high voice:

"*Master, mock on; the scorn thou givest me,*

"*Pray Jove, some lady may return on thee.*"

The Second Pyrgus said, "No, you shall see me do the Moor."

He said to Tucca, "Master, lend me your scarf for a little while."

The scarf was an English officer's sash.

The Second Pyrgus was going to recite some dialogue from George Peele's *The Battle of Alcazar*; the sash would be used for the turban of the Moor Muly Mahamet.

"Here," Tucca said, handing over the scarf. "It is at thy service, boy."

The Second Pyrgus said, "You, Master Minos, hark hither a little. Come here and let's talk."

He drew Minos to the side and spoke to him.

Minos and the Second Pyrgus then withdrew to make themselves ready for the scene.

Tucca said to Histrio, "How do thou like him? Are thou not rapt? Are thou not tickled, now? Don't thou applaud, rascal? Don't thou applaud?"

"Yes," Histrio said. "What will you ask for them to act for a week, Captain?"

Tucca answered:

"No, you mangonizing slave, I will not part from them; you'll sell them for ingles, you will."

"Mangonizing" means "trafficking in slaves," and one meaning of "ingle" is a boy used for homosexual purposes.

Tucca continued talking, this time about the guests for the upcoming supper to be hosted by Histrio:

"Let's have good cheer tomorrow night at supper, stalker, and then we'll talk. Good capon and plover, do you hear, sirrah? And do not bring your eating actor with you there; I cannot tolerate him; he will eat a leg of mutton while I am still eating my porridge, the lean Poluphagos; his belly is like Barathrum, he looks like a midwife in man's apparel, the slave."

Capons and plovers are kinds of fowl.

The words "Poluphagos" and "Barathrum" are related to eating excessively. "Polyphagous" means a voracious eater. "Barathrum" was a deep pit in Athens, Greece; the word is also applied to gluttons with a deep pit for a stomach.

Tucca continued:

"Nor bring with you the villainous out-of-tune fiddler Enobarbus; don't bring him."

"Enobarbus" means "Redbeard."

Tucca then asked:

"How much money have thou there? Six-and-thirty, huh?"

Histrio replied, "No, here's all I have, Captain: some five-and-twenty."

He gave Tucca the money and said:

"Please, sir, will you present and accommodate — give it in a way appropriate to him — to the gentleman?

"For my own part, I am a mere stranger to his humor — I have no idea how to appropriately give him the money.

"Besides, I have some business that invites me away from here, with Master Asinius Lupus, the Tribune."

Tucca said:

"Well, go thy ways, pursue thy projects; let me alone with this design."

A design is 1) a plan, or 2) a trick.

The trick might be to keep the money for himself and not give it to Crispinus.

Tucca continued:

"My poetaster shall make thee a play, and thou shall be a man of good parts in it."

"A man of good parts" can mean 1) a character with good qualities, or 2) an actor with many good parts. Actors sometimes performed more than one role in plays.

Tucca again considered the guest list:

"But wait, let me see: Do not bring your Aesop, your 'politician' who deals with officials, unless you can ram up his mouth with sweet-smelling cloves; the slave smells ranker than some sixteen dunghills and is seventeen times more rotten.

"By the Virgin Mary, you may bring Frisker, a zany clown; he's a good skipping swaggerer; and your fat fool there, my Mango, bring him, too —"

"Mango" means "Pimp" in this context.

Tucca continued:

"— but don't let him beg rapiers or scarves from the audience in his over-familiar playing face to use in his comic sketches, nor roar out his barren bold jests with a tormenting laughter, between drunk and dry, aka sober.

"Do you hear, Stifftoe? Give him warning, admonition, to forsake his saucy insolence and glavering — deceitful flattering — grace and his goggle eye; it does not become him, sirrah; tell him so.

"I have stood up and defended you, I, to gent'men, when you have been said to prey upon puisnes — naïve youths — and honest citizens for socks or boots to use in a play, or when they have called you usurers or brokers, or said you were able to help someone to a piece of flesh — a prostitute; I have sworn to these accusers that I did not think so.

"Nor that you were the common retreats for punks — prostitutes — decayed in the practice of their trade. I cannot believe it of you —"

Actually, Captain Tucca was one of many who brought prostitutes to see plays.

Histrio said, "Thank you, Captain. May Jupiter and the rest of the gods confine your modern delights without disgust!"

Histrio was wishing that the gods would show favor to Tucca: to let him continue indulging in his delights without him becoming sated — bored — with them.

Histrio started to leave.

Tucca said:

"Wait, thou shall see one of my Pyrgi play the Moor before thou go."

Demetrius entered the scene.

Tucca asked:

"Who's he with the half arms there, who salutes us out of his cloak like a motion, huh?"

"Half arms" may mean that the elbows of his clothes were torn and covered up by his cloak. His efforts to keep the holes covered meant that he kept the upper half of his arms inside his cloak.

A "motion" is a puppet.

Histrio said:

"Oh, sir, his doublet's a little decayed, a little worn out; he is otherwise a very simple, honest fellow, sir, one Demetrius, a dresser of plays about the town here."

A doublet is a man's upper garment: a jacket.

Dressers wrote, adapted, and modified plays. They worked often with collaborators.

Histrio continued:

"We have hired him to abuse Horace and make him a character in a play with all his gallants, such as Tibullus, Maecenas, Cornelius Gallus, and the rest."

"And why so, stinkard?" Tucca said.

"Oh, it will get us a huge deal of money, Captain, and we have need of it, for this winter has made us all poorer than so many starved snakes," Histrio said. "Nobody comes to attend our plays: not a gentleman, nor a —"

Possibly, he was going to say "prostitute."

Tucca interrupted, "— but you know nothing about Horace, do you, to make a play about him?"

"Indeed, not much, Captain," Histrio said, "but our author — Demetrius — will devise something that shall serve in some fashion."

Tucca said:

"Why, my Parnassus here shall help him if thou want."

Parnassus is a mountain sacred to the Muses. Tucca was using the word as a name for Crispinus.

Tucca then asked:

"Can thy author do it impudently enough?"

"Oh, I promise you, Captain, he can, and spitefully enough, too," Histrio said. "He has one of the most overflowing rank wits in Rome. He will slander any man who breathes, if he is disgusted by him."

Tucca said:

"I'll know the poor, egregious, nitty rascal, if he has these commendable qualities."

"Nitty" means "infested with nits" — the eggs of lice.

Tucca continued:

"I'll cherish him — wait, here comes the Tartar — I'll make a gathering for him, I will: a purse of money, and put the poor slave in fresh rags."

A purse is a container for money.

In slang, a Tartar is a thief or beggar.

The "poor slave" was Demetrius.

The Tartar is a character whom the Second Pyrgus would perform.

Since the Tartar is a tall character, the Second Pyrgus was sitting on Minos' shoulders.

Tucca said to Histrio, "Tell him — tell Demetrius — about the purse of money, to comfort him."

He then said to the Second Pyrgus, "Well done, boy."

The Second Pyrgus recited:

"Where art [are] thou, boy? Where is Calipolis [the Tartar's wife]?

"Fight, earthquakes, in the entrails of the earth,

"And eastern whirlwinds in the hellish shades!

"Some foul contagion of the infected heavens

"Blast all the trees, and in their cursed tops

"The dismal night-raven and tragic owl

"Breed, and become forerunners of my fall!"

Tucca said to Histrio:

"Well, now fare thee well, my honest penny-biter."

Tucca was saying that Histrio was an honest collector of the fees for seeing the play from audience members. He would bite a penny to make sure it was genuine.

Tucca continued:

"Commend me to Seven-shares-and-a-half — the majority share-holder — and remember tomorrow's supper. If you lack a service, you shall play in my name, rascals, but you shall buy your own clothing, and I'll have two shares for my countenance — my patronage."

He would be the patron — the sponsor — of the company.

By statute, actors could be charged with being rogues or vagabonds unless their acting troupe had a high-ranking member of society as its patron.

Histrio and Demetrius started to exit, but Tucca said to Histrio, "Let thy author stay with me."

Demetrius, the author, said to Tucca, "Yes, sir. "

Histrio exited.

Tucca said to Minos, "It was well done, little Minos, thou did stalk well. Forgive me that I said thou stunk, Minos; it was the savor of a poet I met sweating in the street, the stink hangs yet in my nostrils."

Crispinus asked, "Who was it? Horace?"

"Aye, it was he," Tucca said. "Do thou know him?"

"Oh, he forsook me most barbarously, I declare," Crispinus said.

Tucca said, "Hang him, the fusty- and stale-smelling satyr, he smells all of goat; he carries a ram under his armholes, the slave. I am the worse when I see him."

Tucca and Crispinus then spoke quietly together a little distance from Minos and Demetrius.

Tucca asked, "Did Minos impart money to you?"

Showing Tucca the money, Crispinus said, "Yes, here are twenty drachmas he did convey to me."

Hmm. Drachmas? More likely, sesterces. Unless Minos was suddenly generous.

Tucca said, "Well said. Keep them; we'll share soon."

He then said loudly, "Come, little Minos."

Crispinus said, "Indeed, Captain, I'll be bold to show you a mistress of mine, a woman to whom I pay attention, a jeweler's wife, a gallantly and fashionably dressed woman, as we go along."

Tucca replied:

"There spoke my genius — my guardian spirit. Minos, some of thy eringoes, little Minos, send them to us."

Eringoes were supposed to be aphrodisiacs. Tucca wanted to be prepared, just in case he needed to be prepared.

Tucca said to Crispinus:

"Come hither, Parnassus."

He indicated Demetrius and said:

"I must have thee become familiar with my little locust — Demetrius — here; it is a good vermin, they say."

He looked around and said:

"Look, here's Horace and old Trebatius, the great lawyer, in his company. Let's avoid him now; he is too well seconded."

In other words, Horace had too strong a supporter to be approached now.

Horace the poet and Trebatius the lawyer spoke together. Their conversation consisted of a defense of poetry and satire, and it was rhymed.

Horace said:

"There are those to whom I seem excessively sour,

"And past a satire's law seem to extend my power;

"[And seem to extend my power past a satire's law;]

"Others, who think whatever I have writ [written]

"Wants pith and matter to eternise it,

"[Lacks force and content to make it eternal,]

"And that they could in one day's light disclose [to the world]

"A thousand verses such as I compose."

Horace, Virgil, and Ben Jonson were all criticized for writing slowly.

Horace then asked:

"What shall I do, Trebatius? Tell me."

Trebatius answered:

"Surcease. [Stop.]"

Horace said:

"And shall my muse admit no more increase?

"[And shall my muse allow no more writing of satire?]"

Trebatius answered:

"So I advise."

Horace said:

"An ill death let me die

"If it were not best;

"[Let me die a bad death if I don't agree that your advice is best;]

"but sleep avoids my eye,

"And I use [the time to write] these [verses], lest nights should tedious seem."

Trebatius said:

"Rather contend to sleep, and live like them

"Who, holding golden sleep in special price,

"Rubbed with sweet oils, swim silver Tiber thrice,

"And every evening with neat wine steeped be."

Trebatius was advising Horace to court sleep by being rubbed with oil before engaging in the vigorous exercise of swimming back and forth across the Tiber River three times, and drinking wine.

Trebatius said:

"Or, if such love of writing ravish thee,

"Then dare to sing unconquered Caesar's deeds,

"Who cheers such actions with abundant meeds [rewards]."

Trebatius was advising Horace that if he didn't like the first advice he had been given, then he could instead praise Augustus Caesar in his poetry — Augustus Caesar rewarded such writing.

Horace said:

"That, father, I desire."

Tiberius was older than Horace, and Horace used the word "father" as a title of respect.

Horace continued:

"But when I try,

"I feel defects in every faculty [capacity].

"Nor is it a labor fit for every pen

"To paint the horrid troops of armed men,

"The lances burst in Gallia's slaughtered forces,

"Or wounded Parthians tumbled from their horses.

"Great Caesar's wars cannot be fought with words."

Gallia and Parthia are geographical locations.

Praise of Augustus Caesar would involve praise of his generalship and his military victories, something that Horace did not think his skills were suited to do.

Trebatius said:

"Yet what his virtue in his peace affords,

"His fortitude and justice, thou can show,

"As wise Lucilius honored Scipio."

Gaius Lucilius, the father of Roman satire, was a poet who wrote about and honored Scipio Aemilianus, a general who oversaw the defeat and destruction of Carthage in the third and final Punic War.

Horace replied:

"Of that my powers shall suffer no neglect,

"When such slight labors may aspire [to] respect."

In other words: I will endeavor to do so, since such slight works may hope to be recognized.

Horace continued:

"But if I watch not a most chosen time,

"The humble words of Flaccus cannot climb

"The attentive ear of Caesar."

Horace's name was Quintus Horatius Flaccus. He worried that even if he wrote poetry praising Augustus Caesar, the Roman Emperor might not become aware of it.

Horace continued:

"Nor must I

"With less observance shun gross flattery,

"For he, reposed safe in his own merit,

"Spurns back the glozes [smooth deceiving compliments] of a fawning [flattering] spirit."

Horace was aware that if he wrote such praising poetry, he must be careful not to overdo the praise because Augustus Caesar disliked fawning flattery.

Trebatius said:

"But how much better would such accents sound

"Than with a sad and serious verse to wound

"Pantolabus, railing in his saucy jests?

"Or Nomentanus, spent [exhausted] in riotous feasts?

"In satires, each man (though untouched) complains

"As [if] he were hurt, and hates such biting strains."

Pantolabus was a buffoon, and Nomentanus was a spendthrift. In real life, Horace satirized both.

Horace replied:

"What shall I do? Milonius shakes his heels

"In ceaseless dances when his brain once feels

"The stirring fervor of the wine ascend

"And that his eyes false number apprehend

"Castor his horse, Pollux loves handy fights;

"[Where there are] A thousand heads, [there are also] a thousand choice delights.

"My pleasure is in feet my words to close,

"As, both our better, old Lucilius does."

In other words:

People follow their passions.

Milonius loves to get drunk and dance. Castor loves his horses. Pollux loves to fight hand to hand in boxing matches.

Horace loves to write satires like his inspiration, old Lucilius, who is superior to both Horace and Trabatius, and Horace loves to put his words in metrical feet.

Horace continued:

"He as his trusty friends his books did trust

"With all his secrets, nor in things unjust

"Or actions lawful ran to other men."

Lucilius put his secrets, good or bad, in his books, treating them like trustworthy friends. Because he did that in books, he did not need to confide those things to other men.

Horace continued:

"So that the old man's life described was seen

"As in a votive table, in his lines."

A votive table is a panel with an image of a danger that has been survived. People would make vows in times of danger, such as illness or shipwreck. When they had survived the danger and fulfilled the vow, they would hang a votive table in a sacred place such as a church.

Horace continued:

"And to his [Lucilius'] steps my genius inclines,

"Lucanian or Apulian, I not whether [I don't know which],

"For the Venusian colony plows either,"

In other words: Horace's guardian spirit has guided him and shaped his character to make him want to write satire. Of course, our environment helps shape our character. Horace came from Venusia, which was settled by farmers and other people from Lucania and Apulia.

Horace continued:

"Sent thither when the Sabines were forced thence

"(As old fame sings), to give the place defense

"'gainst such as, seeing it empty, might make road [inroads, aka raids]

"Upon the empire, or there fix abode —

"Whether the Apulian borderer it were

"Or the Lucanian violence they fear."

The Romans captured Venusia from the Sabines, and then the Romans settled loyal-to-Rome people from Lucania and Apulia in Venusia lest people hostile to Rome settled there. This helped prevent raids by enemies into Roman territory.

Horace continued:

"But this my style no living man shall touch

"If first I am not forced by base reproach;

"But, like a sheathed sword, it [my style and my writing instrument] shall defend

"My innocent life."

In other words:

Horace is a defender, not an attacker. He will defend himself in his satire if he is attacked, but he will not attack first. His pointed writing instrument is like a sheathed sword: When needed, it can become a dangerous weapon. Because people know that, chances are they will leave him alone.

The Latin word *stylus* can mean 1) style, 2) sword, and 3) pointed writing instrument.

Horace continued:

"For why should I contend [strive]

"To draw it out, when no malicious thief

"Robs my good name, the treasure of my life?

"O Jupiter, let it with rust be eaten

"Before it touch or insolently threaten

"The life of any with the least disease [disquiet];

"So much I love and woo a general peace.

"But he who wrongs me, better, I proclaim,

"He never had assayed to touch my fame [reputation].

"For he shall weep, and walk with every tongue

"Throughout the city infamously sung."

In other words: If you attack me with libel and slander, I will attack you with satire.

Horace continued:

"Servius the Praetor threats [threatens] the laws and urn

"If any at his deeds repine or spurn;

"The witch Canidia, that Albucius got [begot],

"Denounceth [Proclaims] witchcraft where she loves not;

"Thurius the judge does thunder worlds of ill

"To such as strive with his judicial will.

"All men affright [frighten] their foes in what they may;

"Nature commands it, and men must obey."

In other words: People defend themselves with what weapons they have. A Praetor can threaten to defend himself with laws and urns — jurors would place votes of guilty or not guilty in an urn. A witch can threaten to defend herself with witchcraft. A judge can threaten to defend himself by giving a heaping helping of hurt to his enemies.

Horace continued:

"Observe with me: The wolf his tooth does use,

"The bull his horn[s]. And who does this infuse

"But Nature?"

In other words: Who but Nature inspires these threats against enemies?

Horace continued:

"There's luxurious Scaeva; [en]trust

"His long-lived mother with him, his so just

"And scrupulous right hand no mischief will,

"No more than with his heel a wolf will kill,

"Or [an] ox with jaw. Marry [By the Virgin Mary], [if you] let him alone

"With tempered [mixed] poison to remove [he will kill] the crone."

In other words: Scaeva likes luxuries and is waiting for his aged mother to die so he can get her inheritance. His right hand will do her no harm, just as a wolf will do no harm with a heel or an ox will do no harm with a jaw. But a wolf has jaws and an ox has horns, and Scaeva has a sinister — left — hand that will serve poison to her quickly if he has the opportunity.

Horace continued:

"But briefly: If to age I destined be,

"Or that quick death's black wings environ [wrap around] me;
"If rich, or poor; at Rome, or fate command
"I shall be banished to some other land;
"What hue soever my whole state shall bear,
"I will write satires still, in spite of fear."

In other words: Whether I live for a long time or I live for a short time, whether I live at Rome or I am exiled, whether I have a not-dark, fortunate life or a dark, unfortunate life, I will always write satires, even if I am afraid of the effects of doing so.

Trebatius replied:

"Horace, I fear thou draw'st no lasting breath,
"And that some great man's friend will be thy death."

In other words: I am afraid that you won't live long, and that having Lucilius, the friend of Scipio Aemilianus, aka Scipio Africanus the Younger, as your satiric influence will result in your death.

Horace said:

"What? When the man who first did satirize
"Durst [dared] pull the skin over the ears of vice
"And make who stood in outward fashion clear
"Give place, as foul within, shall I forbear?"

In other words: My satiric influence, Lucilius, the father of Roman satire, did such things as metaphorically flay the ears of a man of vice and show that a man who appeared to be good was actually bad. If he was able to do such things, should I decide not to do them out of fear?

Horace continued:

"Did Laelius, or the man so great with fame
"That [Who] from sacked Carthage fetched his worthy name,
"Storm that Lucilius did Metellus pierce
"Or bury Lupus quick in famous verse?"

In other words: Gaius Laelius was a soldier and consul who was called *Sapiens*, aka "the Wise." He was friends with Scipio Amelianus, aka Scipio Africanus Minor (the Younger), a Roman hero of the Third Punic War against Carthage in North Africa. Neither of them objected when Lucilius satirized Metellus or Lupus. Metellus was a Censor; he and Scipio disagreed about some things, but without animosity. Lucius Cornelius Lentulus Lupus, who was

Consul in 156 BCE, was metaphorically buried quick — alive — by Lucilius' satire.

Lucilius died in 103 BCE.

Horace's life dates are 65 BCE to 8 CE.

Augustus Caesar reigned as Roman Emperor from 27 BCE. to 14 CE.

Horace continued:

"Rulers and subjects by whole tribes he checked,

"But virtue and her friends did still protect."

In other words: Lucilius satirized both the high-born and the low-born, but he always protected virtuous people.

Horace continued:

"And when from sight or from the judgment seat

"The virtuous Scipio and wise Laelius met

"Unbraced with him, in all light sports [entertainments] they shared,

"Till their most frugal suppers were prepared."

In other words: Scipio and Laelius often met with Lucilius in private, where they relaxed — unbraced themselves — and had a meal together.

Horace continued:

"Whatever I am, though both for wealth and wit

"Beneath Lucilius I am pleased to sit,

"Yet Envy, [in] spite of her empoisoned breast,

"Shall say I lived in grace [in favor] here with the best;

"And, seeking in weak trash [worthless people] to make her wound,

"Shall find me solid [impervious], and her teeth unsound —

"'less learned Trebatius' censure disagree."

In other words:

Horace was OK with being honored less than Lucilius both for wealth and wit, and he was willing to sit lower at the supper table than him: Lucilius would have the seat of honor.

Horace would still have a very good life, and malicious Envy would be able to do him no harm.

Nevertheless, he wanted to hear his friend Trebatius' opinion and whether it opposed his view.

Trebatius replied:

"No, Horace, I of force [I by the force of your strong arguments] must yield to thee.

"Only take heed, as being advised by me,

"Lest thou incur some danger. Better pause

"Than rue thy ignorance of the sacred laws;

"There's justice, and great action may be sued

"'gainst such as wrong men's fames with verses lewd."

Trebatius agreed that Horace must follow his Muse and write satire, but he advised Horace to be careful about libeling anyone in his writing. Writing libelous verses could result in great legal punishments.

"Lewd" meant 1) evil, and 2) bungling.

Horace said:

"Aye, with lewd verses such as libels be,

"And aimed at persons of good quality;

"I reverence and adore that just decree.

"But if they shall be sharp yet modest rhymes

"That spare men's persons and but just tax [attack only] their crimes,

"Such shall in open court find current pass

"Were Caesar judge, and with the Maker's grace."

In other words: Yes, libelous satire ought to be punished, but good satire whose target is a crime or sin instead of a person is legal. This is true even if Augustus Caesar were the judge, and such attacks against crimes and sins meet with the Creator's — God's — favor.

Trebatius said:

"Nay, I'll add more: If thou thyself being clear

"Shall tax in person a man fit to bear

"Shame and reproach, his suit shall quickly be

"Dissolved in laughter, and thou thence set free."

In other words: Let me add that if you satirize a man who is disreputable and notorious, the lawsuit will quickly be thrown out of court and you will be free.

In Horace's society, anyone who wanted to be cleared of imputations of criminal behavior first had to provide character witnesses and other evidence that he was a man of good character.

CHAPTER 4

— 4.1 —

Chloe and Cytheris talked together in a room in Albius and Chloe's house. With them were one or two maids carrying a muff, a dog, a fan, and a mask.

"But, sweet lady, tell me, am I well enough attired for the court, seriously?" Chloe asked.

"Well enough?" Cytheris said. "Excellent well, sweet Mistress Chloe. This strait-bodied — tight-fitting — city attire, I can tell you, will stir a courtier's blood more than the finest loose sacks the ladies are accustomed to be put in."

"Loose sacks" are loosely fitting dresses.

Cytheris added, "And then you are as well jeweled as any of them; your ruff and linen about you is much more pure white than theirs; and as for your beauty, I can tell you, there's many of them who would defy the painter — the cosmetician — if they could exchange looks with you. By the Virgin Mary, the worst thing is, you must look to be envied and endure a few court frumps — jeers — for it."

"Oh, Jove, madam, I shall buy them too cheap!" Chloe said.

In other words: Enduring a few jeers is a small price to pay for triumphs in fashionable company.

Jove is Jupiter, King of the gods.

Chloe ordered a maid, "Give me my muff and my dog there."

Fashionable ladies carried a muff and a dog.

Chloe then said to Cytheris, "And will the ladies be at all friendly with me, do you think?"

"Oh, Juno!" Cytheris said.

Juno is the wife of Jupiter, King of the gods.

She continued, "Why, you shall see them flock about you with their puff wings and ask you where you bought your lawn, and what you paid for it, who starches you — and entreat you to help them to some pure laundresses out of the city."

Puff wings are pieces of cloth that hide the join between a sleeve and the body of a garment. Sometimes fashionable people slashed the upper layer of material and pulled out some of the lower layer of material to create a puff.

Lawn was an expensive linen fabric.

Laundresses washed and starched clothing and kept white fabric white.

"Oh, Cupid!" Chloe said.

She ordered a maid, "Give me my fan, and my mask, too."

Fashionable ladies also carried around a fan and a mask.

She then asked Cytheris, "And will the lords and the poets there treat one well, too, lady?"

Cytheris said:

"Don't doubt that.

"You shall have kisses from them go pit-pat, pit-pat, pit-pat upon your lips as thick as stones out of slings at the assault of a city.

"And your ears will be so furred with the breath of their compliments that you cannot catch cold in your head even if you wanted to, for three winters afterward."

In other words: Compliments whispered in her ears would keep her ears so warm that she would be unable to catch cold.

"Thank you, sweet lady," Chloe replied. "Oh, heaven! And how must one behave herself among them? You know all."

Cytheris answered:

"Indeed, one must behave impudently enough, Mistress Chloe, and well enough.

"Carry not too much underthought — deference — between yourself and them; nor your city-mannerly word 'forsooth.' Don't use it too often in any case, but instead say plain 'aye, madam' and 'no, madam.' Nor never say 'Your Lordship' nor 'Your Honor,' but 'you,' and 'you, my lord' and 'my lady'; the other they count too simple and minsitive — too mincing sensitive and too humble and affected.

"And although they desire to kiss heaven with their titles, yet they will account as fools those who give them too humbly and deferentially."

"Oh, intolerable! Jupiter!" Chloe said. "By my truth, lady, I would not for a world have missed out on you staying in my house; and indeed you shall not pay a farthing for your board nor your chambers."

“Oh, sweet Mistress Chloe!” Cytheris said.

“Indeed, you shall not, lady,” Chloe said.

Cytheris started to speak, but Chloe said, “Nay, good lady, do not offer it.”

Gallus and Tibullus entered the scene. They were elegiac poets.

"Come, where are these ladies?" Gallus said. "With your permission, bright stars, this gentleman and I have come to man you — escort you — to court, where your recent kind entertainment is now to be requited with a heavenly banquet."

The recent kind entertainment was the buffet that Chloe and Albius had hosted.

"A heavenly banquet, Gallus?" Cytheris said.

"No less, my dear Cytheris," Gallus said.

Tibullus said, "That would not be strange, lady, if the epithet of 'heavenly' were only given for the company invited thither: yourself and" — indicating Chloe — "this fair gentlewoman."

"Are we invited to court, sir?" Chloe asked.

"You are, lady," Tibullus said, "by the great princess Julia, who longs to greet you with any favors that may worthily make you an often — a frequent — courtier."

"In sincerity, I thank her, sir," Chloe said. "You have a coach, haven't you?"

"The princess has sent her own, lady," Tibullus said.

"Oh, Venus! That's well," Chloe said. "I do long to ride in a coach most vehemently."

"But, sweet Gallus, please explain to me why you give that heavenly praise to this earthly banquet?" Cytheris asked.

"Because, Cytheris, it must be celebrated by the heavenly powers," Gallus answered. "All the gods and goddesses will be there; to two of which you two must be exalted."

"A pretty fiction, in truth," Chloe said.

"A fiction indeed, Chloe, and fit for the fit of a poet," Cytheris said.

"Fit" can mean 1) suitable, 2) a poetic episode of inspiration, and 3) a section of a poem or song.

Gallus said, "Why, Cytheris, may not poets, from whose divine spirits all the honors of the gods have been deduced, entreat so much honor of the gods to have their divine presence at a poetical banquet?"

Gallus was referring to the belief that poets were the first priests because they were the first to praise and honor the gods.

"Suppose that to be no fiction," Cytheris said, "yet where are your abilities to make us two goddesses at your feast?"

"Who doesn't know, Cytheris, that the sacred breath of a true poet can blow any virtuous humanity up to deity?" Gallus answered.

Tibullus said:

"To tell you the female truth (which is the simple, uncomplicated truth), ladies, and to show that poets, in spite of the world, are able to deify themselves, at this banquet to which you are invited, we intend to assume the figures of the gods, and to give our various loves the forms of goddesses.

"Ovid will be Jupiter; the Princess Julia will be Juno; Gallus here will be Apollo; you, Cytheris, will be Pallas Athena, goddess of wisdom; I will be Bacchus; and my love, Plautia, will be Ceres."

Bacchus is the god of grapes, and Ceres is the goddess of grain. The god of wine and the goddess of food are appropriate deities for a banquet.

Tibullus continued:

"And to install you and your husband, fair Chloe, in honors equal with ours, you shall be a goddess and your husband shall be a god."

"A god?" Chloe said. "O my god!"

"A god, but a lame god, lady," Tibullus said, "for he shall be Vulcan, and you shall be Venus, and this will make our banquet no less than heavenly."

Venus cuckolded Vulcan.

"In sincerity, it will be sugared — it will be a treat," Chloe said. "Good Jove, what a pretty foolish thing it is to be a poet!"

She then said quietly to Cytheris, "But listen, sweet Cytheris: couldn't they possibly leave out my husband? I think a body's husband does not so well at court; a person's friend or lover, or such, will do well — but a husband, it is like your clog to your marmoset, for all the world and the heavens."

A marmoset is a monkey. Its leg or neck could be affixed to a clog — a block of wood — that would restrict its movement.

Chloe did not want her husband to restrict her movements at the party.

Cytheris replied, "Tut, never fear, Chloe; your husband will be left outside in the lobby or the great chamber, when you shall be put in in the closet — private room — by this lord and by that lady."

This, of course, would provide an opportunity for Chloe's husband, Albus, to be cuckolded.

"Then I am reassured," Chloe said. "My husband shall go."

Horace entered the scene.

"Horace! Welcome," Gallus said.

"Gentlemen, did you hear the news?" Horace asked.

"What news, my Quintus?" Tibullus asked.

Horace's name was Quintus Horatius Flaccus.

Horace answered, "Our melancholic friend, Propertius, has enclosed himself in his Cynthia's tomb, and he will by no entreaties be drawn away from there."

Albius arrived and ushered in Crispinus, Tucca, and Demetrius.

"Good Master Crispinus, please bring the gentleman near," Albius said.

The gentleman was Tucca.

Horace said to his companions, "Crispinus? Hide me, good Gallus; Tibullus, shelter me!"

Crispinus said to Tucca, "Make your approach, sweet Captain."

"What does this mean, Horace?" Tibullus asked.

Horace said to his companions, "I am surprised — ambushed — again; farewell."

"Stay, Horace," Gallus requested.

Horace replied, "What, and be tired on — that is, attacked and torn at — by yonder vulture? No, Phoebus defend me!"

Horace exited — quickly.

"By God's light!" Tibullus said. "I hold my life this is the same man who met him in Holy Street."

Of course, that man was Crispinus.

"Indeed, it is likely enough," Gallus said.

He then said, "This act of Propertius seems very strange to me."

Tucca said to Crispinus, "By thy leave, my neat scoundrel. What! Is this the mad boy you talked about?"

One kind of "mad boy" in Ben Jonson's society was the "roaring boy." They were fashionable men who liked to argue, bully, and fight. Of course, Albius was not a roaring boy.

Crispinus answered, "Aye, this is Master Albius, Captain."

Tucca said to Albius, "Give me thy hand, Agamemnon; we hear abroad thou are the Hector of citizens. What do thou say? Are we welcome to thee, noble Neoptolemus?"

Agamemnon was the leader of the Greeks against the Trojans in the Trojan War. Neoptolemus was the son of Achilles, a Greek who was the greatest warrior in the Trojan War. Hector was the greatest Trojan warrior.

Albius said, "Welcome, Captain! By Jove and all the gods in the Capitol —"

"No more; we conceive thee," Tucca said. "Which of these is thy wedlock, Menelaus? Thy Helen? Thy Lucrece? So that we may do her honor, mad boy?"

"Thy wedlock" means "your wife."

Menelaus was the King of Sparta, whose wife, Helen, after being forcibly kidnapped by or voluntarily running away with Paris, Prince of Troy, became Helen of Troy.

Lucrece was an ancient Roman gentlewoman who committed suicide after being raped. The son of King Tarquin of Rome, who was also named Tarquin, raped her. After her suicide, King Tarquin was overthrown. Rome ceased to be a kingdom and instead became a republic.

Tucca was comparing Albius to Menelaus, a wronged husband, and he was comparing Albius' wife, Chloe, to Helen and Lucrece, two women connected with unethical sex.

Tucca wanted to seduce Chloe.

"She in the little fine dressing, sir, is my mistress," Crispinus said.

By "mistress," he meant a woman he served and was devoted to.

"For lack of a better, sir," Albius said.

Tucca said, "A better, profane rascal?"

He then said, "I ask thee mercy, my good scroil, was it thou who said that?"

"Scroil" is Tucca-speak for "scoundrel."

"No harm, Captain," Albius said.

"She is a Venus, a Vesta, a Melpomene!" Tucca said.

Venus is the goddess of sexual passion. Vesta is the goddess of the hearth. Melpomene is the goddess of tragedy.

Tucca said to Chloe, "Come hither, Penelope."

Penelope is the faithful wife of Odysseus, both of whom are in Homer's *Odyssey*. Odysseus' Roman name is Ulysses.

Tucca and Chloe talked together a short distance away from the others.

"What's thy name, Iris?" Tucca asked.

Iris is the goddess of the rainbow; she is a messenger-goddess.

"My name is Chloe, sir. I am a gentlewoman."

"Thou are in merit to be an Empress, Chloe, for an eye and a lip," Tucca said. "Thou have an Emperor's nose."

The Roman Emperor was Augustus Caesar.

A Roman nose is large.

He kissed her and said, "Kiss me again."

She kissed him.

He said, "It is a virtuous punk."

One meaning of "punk" is "prostitute." Now that Chloe, a married woman, has kissed him, he will call her that often.

Tucca said, "Good. Before Jove, the gods were a sort of goslings when they suffered so sweet a breath to perfume the bed of a stinkard. Thou had ill fortune, Thisbe; the Fates were infatuate; they were, punk, they were."

He was already criticizing her husband to her.

Thisbe and Pyramus were lovers. Thisbe ran away from home to marry Pyramus. She saw a lion with blood on its mouth from hunting, and she ran away from it, leaving her cloak behind. The lion tore the cloak, getting blood on it. A little later, seeing the bloody cloak, Pyramus thought that Thisbe had been killed by the lion, and he committed suicide. She found his body, and she committed suicide.

"Infatuate" means "infatuated" as an adjective.

"Infatuated" can mean "utterly foolish."

As a verb, "infatuate" can mean "make people foolish."

Possibly, Tucca meant that the fates of Thisbe and Pyramus were foolish. In other words: It is foolish to commit suicide because of love. In addition, according to Tucca, the Fates, who are usually portrayed as old women, were being utterly foolish in giving Pyramus and Thisbe this fate. "Foolish" is the opposite of what the Fates usually are.

Meanwhile, Propertius was in the tomb of his lover. We shall hear no more about him. His friends were getting ready to party.

"That's sure, sir," Chloe said. "Let me crave — have — your name, I ask you, sir."

"I am known by the name of Captain Tucca, punk; the noble Roman, punk; a gent'man and a commander, punk," Tucca said.

"In good time!" Chloe said.

She thought that she was fortunate to meet him.

She continued, "A gentleman and a commander? That's as good as a poet, I think."

She walked aside.

Crispinus picked up a viol and said, "A pretty instrument!"

A viol is a kind of stringed musical instrument.

He asked Albius, "It's my cousin Cytheris' viol, this is, isn't it?"

Cytheris said to Crispinus, "Play, cousin, play it. It lacks only such a voice and hand to grace it as yours is."

"Alas, cousin, you are merrily inspired," Crispinus said.

"Please play, if you love me," Cytheris said.

"Yes, cousin," Crispinus replied. "You know I do not hate you."

Tibullus said to Gallus, "A most subtle, cunning wench! How she has baited him with a viol yonder, for a song!"

Crispinus said to Cytheris, "Cousin, please call Mistress Chloe; she shall hear an essay — an example — of my poetry."

"I'll call her," Tucca said.

He approached Chloe and said, "Come hither, cockatrice; here's one who will set thee up, my sweet punk — set thee up."

In other words, he will praise you in song.

"Cockatrice," like "punk," can mean "prostitute."

Chloe said to Crispinus, "Are you a peewit so soon, sir?"

A peewit is a lapwing: its cry is similar to "peewit."

Chloe may have thought the word meant "poet." Or she may have meant that he was a metaphorical songbird.

Albius said, "Wife, be mum."

Crispinus sang:

"Love is blind and a wanton;

"In the whole world, there is scant

　　"One such another;

　　"No, not his mother.

"He has plucked her doves and sparrows
"To feather his sharp arrows,

  "And alone prevaileth
  "Whilst sick Venus waileth.

"But if Cypris once recover
"The wag, it shall behoove her

  "To look better to him,
  "Or she will undo [ruin] him."

"Cypris" is a name for Venus, who had a cult center at Cyprus.

Doves were symbols of love; sparrows were symbols of lust.

Both were birds sacred to Venus.

The song said that Cupid has much power and that Venus may ruin him by giving him too much freedom.

At the soon-to-occur masked party, Ovid (Jupiter) would give the guests much freedom.

Albius said, "Oh, most odoriferous — pleasing — music!"

Tucca said to Albius, "Aha, stinkard! Another Orpheus, you slave, another Orpheus! An Arion riding on the back of a dolphin, rascal!"

Orpheus was a mythical poet and musician. Arion was another mythical poet and musician. According to one story, when pirates threw Arion overboard, a dolphin rescued him and carried him on its back to shore.

Gallus asked Crispinus, "Have you a copy of this ditty, sir?"

"Master Albius has," Crispinus replied.

"Aye, but in truth, they are my wife's verses," Albius said. "I must not show them."

They were the verses of Crispinus, handed to Albius to give to his wife, Chloe.

"Show them, bankrupt, show them," Tucca said. "They have salt in them and will brook the air, stinkard."

The verses have salt — 1) a preservative, and 2) wittiness — in them, and so they can endure the air without being harmed.

Gallus took the verses and read them: "What! '*To his bright mistress, Canidia*'?"

Crispinus, supposed author of the words, said, "Aye, sir, that's just a borrowed name; such as Ovid's Corinna, or Propertius' Cynthia, or your Nemesis or Delia, Tibullus."

Tibullus wrote poems about women whom he named Nemesis and Delia. Delia was his first love, and Nemesis was his last love.

"It's the name of Horace's witch, as I remember," Gallus said.

Canidia is a sorceress in one of Horace's *Satires*.

Tibullus took the verses from Gallus and examined them: "Why, the ditty's all borrowed; it is Horace's! Hang him, the plagiary! He's a plagiarist!"

Crispinus was the plagiarist: He had stolen lines from Horace.

The historical Horace did not write the words. The Horace in Ben Jonson's play is a fictional character somewhat based on the real poet and did not write the words. Ben Jonson wrote this play and so the words are his, and he was called "Horace," a poet whom he loved and respected, in satires about him such as Thomas Dekker's *Satiromastix*.

Tucca said:

"What! He borrow from Horace? He shall pawn himself to ten brokers first."

Tucca was taking Crispinus' side. Either he did not believe that Crispinus was a plagiarist, or he was pretending not to believe that Crispinus was a plagiarist.

Tucca continued:

"Do you hear me, poetasters? I know you to be men of worship."

"Men of worship" are men who are respected.

Tucca then said to the others, "He shall write with Horace for a talent, and let Maecenas and his whole college of critics take his part."

Tucca wanted Horace and Crispinus to compete in a writing contest for a considerable amount of money. Maecenas and his colleagues would be the judges.

Tucca then said to Crispinus, "Thou shall do it, young Phoebus; thou shall, Phaeton; thou shall."

Phaeton went to his father, the god Apollo, and asked to be allowed to drive the Sun-chariot across the sky and bring light to the world. But Phaeton, doomed youth, was unable to control the stallions, and they ran wildly away with the Sun-chariot, wreaking havoc and destruction upon Humankind and the world. The King of the gods, Jupiter, saved Humankind and the world by throwing a thunderbolt at Phaeton and killing him.

Crispinus was being set up for a fall, perhaps unintentionally.

Demetrius, taking Crispinus' side, said to Tucca, "Alas, sir, Horace! He is a mere sponge, nothing but humors and observation; he goes up and down sucking from every society, and when he comes home, he squeezes himself dry again. I know him, I do."

Tucca replied:

"Thou say the truth, my poor poetical fury.

"Horace will pen all he knows. He is a sharp, thorny-toothed, satirical rascal — flee from him. He carries hay in his horn; he will sooner lose his best friend than his least jest."

Farmers tied hay to the horns of dangerous bulls as a warning to people to avoid them.

Tucca continued:

"What Horace once drops on paper against a man lives eternally to upbraid him in the mouth of every slave tankard-bearer or waterman.

"There is not a bawd or a boy who comes from the bakehouse but shall point at him."

The places where people got water and baked goods were also places where they gossiped. According to Tucca, they gossiped about Horace.

Tanker-bearers carried water. Watermen were boatmen.

Tucca continued:

"It is all dog and scorpion; Horace carries poison in his teeth and a sting in his tail.

"Bah, body of Jove! I'll have the slave whipped one of these days for his satires and his humors by one cashiered — discharged — clerk or another."

"We'll undertake — rebuke — him, Captain," Crispinus said.

Demetrius said:

"Aye, and tickle him — beat him — indeed, for his arrogancy and his impudence in commending his own things, and for his translating; I can trace him — trace his sources — indeed."

Ben Jonson used the writing of ancient writers in his own writing, changing things as needed. He did not regard that as plagiarism but as emulation.

The *Oxford English Dictionary* defines the verb "emulate" as "To strive to equal or rival (a person, his achievements or qualities); to copy or imitate with the object of equaling or excelling."

Ben Jonson will emulate Lucian's *Lexiphanes* later in his play when he has a character vomit words.

Demetrius continued:

"Oh, he is the most open fellow living. I had as lief as a new suit I were at it."

In other words, he was as eager to get started as if he were to get a new suit of clothing.

"Open" can mean 1) obvious, and 2) frank and generous.

Tucca said:

"Say no more, then, but do it; it is the only way to get thee a new suit. Sting him, my little newts; I'll give you instructions; I'll be your intelligencer: your informant and spy.

"We'll all join and hang upon him like so many horse-leeches, the actors and all."

Horse-leeches are large leeches; metaphorically, they are parasites.

Tucca continued:

"We shall sup together soon; and then we'll conspire, indeed."

Tucca, Crispinus, Demetrius, and Albius — all conspirators against Horace — walked apart from the others.

Gallus and Tibullus were supporters of Horace.

Gallus said to Tibullus, "Oh, I wish that Horace had stayed and were still here!"

Tibullus replied, "I do not wish that" — he pointed to Crispinus and Demetrius — "because both of these men would have turned Pythagoreans then."

"What, mute?" Gallus asked.

"Aye, as mute as fishes, indeed," Tibullus said.

Pythagorean novices observed a rule of silence.

If Horace were present, Tucca and the others would not be criticizing him.

Tibullus then said to Cytheris and Chloe, "Come, ladies, shall we go?"

"We await you, sir," Cytheris said. "But Mistress Chloe asks if you have not a god to spare" — she pointed to Tucca — "for this gentleman?"

"Who, Captain Tucca?" Gallus asked.

"Aye; he," Cytheris answered.

"Yes, if we can invite him along, he shall be Mars," Gallus said.

"Has Mars anything to do with Venus?" Chloe asked.

Mars had cuckolded Vulcan by sleeping with Vulcan's wife: Venus.

Chloe would be Venus at Julia's entertainment.

"Oh, most of all, lady," Tibullus said.

Chloe said, "Then, I ask to let him be invited. And who shall Crispinus be?"

"Mercury, Mistress Chloe," Tibullus said.

According to one myth, Mercury and Venus were the parents of Cupid. In another myth, Mars was Cupid's father.

"Mercury? That's a poet, isn't it?" Chloe asked.

"No, lady; but somewhat inclining that way," Gallus said.

Mercury was the god of thieves. A plagiarist is a kind of thief.

But Mercury also invented the lyre, and so he invented the musical instrument that poets used to accompany the lyrics they had written.

"He is a herald at arms," Gallus said.

Mercury was a messenger god; medieval heralds carried messages to and from the commanding officers of enemy armies.

"A herald at arms?" Chloe said. "Good. And Mercury? Pretty. He has to do with Venus, too?"

"A little," Tibullus said. "With her face, lady, or so."

Mercury, aka quicksilver, was often used in cosmetic preparations.

"It is very well," Chloe said. "Please, let's go. I long to be at it."

Cytheris said to Crispinus and Tucca, "Gentlemen, shall we ask your companies to come along?"

Crispinus replied, "You shall not only pray, but prevail, lady."

He then said to Tucca, "Come, sweet Captain."

"Yes, I follow," Tucca said.

Tucca then said to Albius, "But thou must not talk of this now, my little bankrupt."

He was referring to the conspiracy against Horace.

Albius said, "Captain, look here."

He put his finger to his lips and said, "Mum."

Demetrius said to Tucca, "I'll go write, sir."

Tucca said:

"Do, do.

"Wait."

He gave Demetrius a coin and said, "Here's a drachma to purchase gingerbread for thy muse."

Everyone exited.

Lupus and Histrio were in a room in Lupus' house, accompanied by a Lictor. Histrio was holding a letter.

Lupus the Tribune said, "Come, let us talk here; here we may be private. Shut the door, Lictor."

He then said to Histrio, "You are an actor, you say."

"Aye, if it pleases Your Worship," Histrio said.

"Good; and how are you able to give this intelligence — this news?" Lupus asked.

"By the Virgin Mary, sir, they directed a letter to me and my fellow sharers in my acting company," Histrio answered.

"Speak lower; you are not now in your theater, stager," Lupus said.

He then said to the First Lictor, "My sword, knave."

The First Lictor fetched Lupus' sword.

Lupus said to Histrio, "They directed a letter to you and your fellow sharers; go forward. Continue."

"Yes, sir," Histrio said. "The purpose of the letter was to hire some of our properties, such as a scepter and a crown for Jove, and a caduceus for Mercury, and a petasus —"

A caduceus is a herald's wand. Mercury carried one that was entwined with two snakes. He also wore a petasus: a hat with a low crown and a wide brim. Mercury often wore a winged hat and/or winged sandals.

Lupus said, "'Caduceus'? And 'petasus'? Let me see your letter."

He took the letter from Histrio and scanned it.

He said, "This is a conjuration — a conspiracy, this is."

Actually, of course, the items were for a costume party.

Lupus then said to the Lictor, "Quickly, on with my buskins!"

The First Lictor fetched Lupus' buskins. Such buskins — boots — were worn by Tribunes and by tragic actors.

The First Lictor helped Lupus put his boots on.

Lupus said to Histrio, "I'll act a tragedy, indeed. Will nothing but our gods serve these poets to profane?"

He said to the First Lictor, "Dispatch! Hurry!"

He then said to Histrio, "Actor, I thank thee. The Emperor shall take knowledge of thy good service. He will be informed."

A knock sounded at the door.

"Who's there now?" Histrio asked.

He then said to the First Lictor, "Look and see who it is, knave."

The First Lictor went to the door.

Lupus re-examined the letter and said, "A crown and a scepter?"

He then said sarcastically, "This is good! Rebellion now?"

The First Lictor returned and said, "It is your apothecary, sir: Master Minos."

Lupus said:

"Why do thou tell me about apothecaries, knave? Tell him I have affairs of state in hand; I can talk to no apothecaries now.

"By the heart of me!

"Stay the apothecary there! Keep him there!"

The First Lictor went to the door.

Lupus said to Histrio:

"You shall see, I have fished out a cunning piece of plot now: They have had some intelligence that their project has been discovered, and now they have arranged with my apothecary to poison me — it is so — knowing that I meant to take medicine today; as sure as death, it is there!

"Jupiter, I thank thee that thou have yet made me so much of a politician."

A politician can be a politic — shrewd — person, in addition to the usual meaning.

Two or more Lictors entered with Minos the apothecary.

Lupus said to Minos, sarcastically, "You are welcome, sir!"

He then said to the Lictors, "Take the potion from him there."

He said to Minos, "I have an antidote more than you know of, sir. "

He said to the Lictors, "Throw it on the ground there."

A Lictor poured the potion onto the floor.

"Good! Now fetch in the dog," Lupus said. "And yet we cannot tarry to try experiments now."

The experiment would have been to have the dog taste the potion. If the dog got sick or died, the potion would be proven to be poisonous. But Lupus was too busy to try the experiment.

Lupus said to the Lictors about Minos, "Arrest him."

The Lictors placed Minos under guard.

Lupus said to Minos, "You shall go with me, sir. I'll tickle you, apothecary; I'll give you a glister, indeed."

A glister is a clyster: an enema or suppository.

He said to himself, "Have I the letter? Aye; it is here."

He then said to the Lictors, "Come, your fasces, Lictors! The half-pikes and the halberds, take them down from the Lares there!"

The fasces were bundles of rods, each bundle containing an axe. Lictors carried them before magistrates as a symbol of the magistrates' power. Half-pikes and halberds are weapons. The Lares were in a lararium: a household shrine devoted to the household gods.

"Actor, assist me!" Lupus said to Histrio.

They armed themselves.

Maecenas and Horace entered the scene.

"Whither now, Asinius Lupus, with this armory?" Maecenas asked.

"I cannot talk now," Lupus said. "I order you, assist me. Treason! Treason!"

"What!" Horace said. "Treason?"

Lupus replied, "Aye; if you love the Emperor and the state, follow me!"

They exited with Minos, who was under guard.

Twelve people in costumes entered a large reception room for Julia's entertainment:

1) Ovid was costumed as Jupiter, King of the gods.

2) Julia was costumed as Juno, Jupiter's wife.

3) Gallus was costumed as Phoebus Apollo, the Sun-god and god of archery.

4) Cytheris was costumed as Pallas Athena, a warrior goddess who was also the goddess of wisdom.

5) Tibullus was costumed as Bacchus, god of grapes and wine.

6) Plautia was costumed as Ceres, goddess of grain and agriculture.

7) Albius was costumed as Vulcan, the blacksmith god.

8) Chloe was costumed as Venus, the goddess of sexual passion.

9) Tucca was costumed as Mars, the god of war.

10) Crispinus was costumed as Mercury, the messenger-god.

11) Hermogenes (the singer) was costumed as Momus, god of ridicule. Momus is a critical fault-finder.

12) A Pyrgus was costumed as Ganymede, a pretty boy who was Jupiter's cupbearer.

The room contained bottles of wine, wine glasses, a table, and chairs to sit on.

Ovid, costumed as Jupiter, and Julia, costumed as Juno, sat at the head of the table.

Ovid (Jupiter) said to the guests:

"Gods and goddesses, take your various seats."

Ovid (Jupiter) then said to Crispinus (Mercury):

"Now, Mercury, move your caduceus and in Jupiter's name command silence."

Crispinus (Mercury) said, "In the name of Jupiter, silence!"

"The crier of the court has too clarified a voice," Hermogenes (Momus) said.

"Clarified" means "pretentious."

The crier of the court was Crispinus (Mercury), who would make announcements as directed by Ovid and Julia.

Hermogenes (Momus) disliked Crispinus (Mercury) because they had recently been rivals in song.

"Peace, Momus," Gallus (Phoebus Apollo) said. "Silence."

"Oh, he is the god of reprehension; let him alone," Ovid (Jupiter) said to Gallus (Phoebus Apollo) about Hermogenes (Momus). "It is his office and his duty."

Momus is the god of ridicule.

Ovid (Jupiter) said to Crispinus (Mercury), "Mercury, go forward and proclaim after Phoebus our high pleasure to all the deities who shall partake of this high banquet."

"Yes, sir," Crispinus (Mercury) replied.

He would repeat the words of Gallus (Phoebus Apollo).

Gallus (Phoebus Apollo) said:

"The great god Jupiter ..."

Crispinus (Mercury) repeated:

"The great god Jupiter ..."

Gallus (Phoebus Apollo) said:

"Of his licentious goodness ..."

Crispinus (Mercury) repeated:

"Of his licentious goodness ..."

Crispinus continued repeating every line after Gallus had spoken it.

Gallus (Phoebus Apollo) said:

"Willing to make this feast no fast from any manner of pleasure, nor to bind any god or goddess to be anything the more god or goddess because of their names, the great god Jupiter gives them all free license to speak no wiser than persons of baser titles and to be nothing better than common men or women.

"And therefore no god shall need to keep himself more strictly to his goddess than any man does to his wife, nor any goddess shall need to keep herself more strictly to her god than any woman does to her husband.

"But since it is no part of wisdom, in these days, to come into bonds, it shall be lawful for every lover to break loving oaths, to change their lovers, and make love to others, as the heat of everyone's blood and the spirit of our nectar shall inspire, and Jupiter save Jupiter!"

Although these banqueters were dressed as gods, they need not act like dignified gods at this banquet.

Nectar is the drink of the gods.

"Heat of blood" can mean "heat of sexual desire."

This was the kind of drinking party at which adultery and cuckolding could take place.

Tibullus (Bacchus) said, "So; now we may play the fools by authority."

Jupiter, King of the gods, had given them permission to be foolish and immoral. Or at least Ovid had.

The company ate and drank.

"To play the fool by authority is wisdom," Hermogenes (Momus) said.

Julia (Juno) said to Hermogenes (Momus), "Away with your mattery sentences, Momus; they are too grave and wise for this meeting."

"Mattery sentences" are maxims with serious matter.

Serious matter was not welcome in this drinking party.

Ovid (Jupiter) pointed to Hermogenes (Momus) and said to Crispinus (Mercury), "Mercury, give our jester a stool; let him sit by, and hand to him some of our delicacies."

Crispinus (Mercury) gave Hermogenes a stool, food, and a cup and made sure he was within reach of good food.

Tucca (Mars) said, "Do thou hear me, mad Jupiter? We'll have it enacted: He who speaks the first wise word shall be made cuckold. What say thou? Isn't it a good motion — a good proposal?"

"Deities, are you all agreed?" Ovid (Jupiter) asked.

All replied, "We are agreed, great Jupiter."

Albius (Vulcan) said, "I have read in a book that to play the fool wisely is high wisdom."

He had said something that could be regarded as wise.

Gallus (Phoebus Apollo) said, "What is this now, Vulcan! Will you be the first wizard?"

A wizard is a wise man.

Ovid (Jupiter) said to Tucca (Mars), "Take his wife, Mars, and make him a cuckold, quickly."

Tucca (Mars) said to Albius' wife, Chloe (Venus), "Come, cockatrice."

Chloe (Venus) said to Ovid (Jupiter) about her husband, "No, let me alone with him, Jupiter — leave him to me."

She then said to Albius (Vulcan), "I'll make you take heed, sir, while you live. I say, if there should be twelve in a company, that you would not be the wisest of them."

There were twelve in this particular company.

Albius (Vulcan) replied, "Say no more; I will not, indeed, wife, hereafter; I'll be here" — he touched his lips — "mum."

Using the royal plural, Ovid (Jupiter) said to the Pyrgus (Ganymede), "Fill for us a bowl of nectar, Ganymede; we will drink to our daughter Venus."

The Pyrgus (Ganymede) poured wine.

Gallus (Phoebus Apollo) said to Albius (Vulcan), "Look after your wife, Vulcan. Pay attention to her. Jupiter begins to court her."

Tibullus (Bacchus) said, "Nay, let Mars look to it; Vulcan must do as Venus does: bear."

Mars was Tucca, who was paying attention to Chloe (Venus), who was ignoring him so she could pay attention to Ovid (Jupiter).

Venus would bear — carry — the weight of a lover in bed; Vulcan would bear — endure — the ignominy of being a cuckold.

Tucca (Phoebus Apollo) said to the Pyrgus (Ganymede), "Sirrah boy; catamite! Look you play Ganymede well now, you slave."

A "catamite" is a boy used for homosexual purposes. The mythological Ganymede was sometimes thought to be a catamite.

Tucca (Phoebus Apollo) continued, "Do not spill your nectar. Carry your cup even; good. You should have rubbed your face with whites of eggs, you rascal, until your brows had shone like our sooty brother's here" — he pointed to Albius (Vulcan, the sooty blacksmith god) — "as sleek as a hornbook, or have steeped your lips in wine until you made them so plump that Juno might have been jealous of them."

The whites of eggs were used as a cosmetic.

Vulcan and Mars are brothers because they are sons of Jupiter and Juno.

Hornbooks were children's primers that were covered with transparent horn, allowing the characters underneath the horn to be read.

"Punk, kiss me, punk," Tucca (Mars) said to Chloe (Venus).

Ovid (Jupiter) took his cup, and to forestall a kiss between Tucca and Chloe, said, "Here, daughter Venus, I drink to thee."

"Thank you, good father Jupiter," Chloe (Venus) said.

Tucca (Mars) said to Julia (Juno), "Why, mother Juno! Gods and fiends! What, will thou endure this ocular temptation?"

Ovid was ogling Chloe.

Juno was a jealous wife.

Tibullus (Bacchus) said, "Mars is enraged; he looks big and begins to sputter for anger."

"Well played, Captain Mars," Hermogenes (Momus) said, happy that Tucca's kiss had been forestalled.

Tucca (Mars) said, "Well said, minstrel Momus; I must put you in, must I? When will you be in good fooling of yourself, fiddler? Never?"

Tucca was asking Hermogenes whether Tucca needed to be the butt of his jokes. Couldn't Hermogenes make better jokes without needing Tucca to be the butt?

This particular drinking party was turning into a burlesque of the gods' banquet at the end of the first book of Homer's *Iliad*. In it, Zeus and Hera (the Roman names are Jupiter and Juno) quarreled, Hephaestus (the Roman name is Vulcan) made jokes to calm the situation, and then they all enjoyed a banquet, followed by listening to music.

Hermogenes (Momus) replied, "Oh, it is our fashion to be silent when there is a better fool in place, always."

"Thank you, rascal," Tucca (Mars) said.

Ovid (Jupiter) said to the Pyrgus (Ganymede), "Fill our cup to honor our daughter Venus, Ganymede. She fills her father with affection."

The Pyrgus continued to serve wine.

"Will thou be ranging, Jupiter, before my face?" Julia (Juno) asked.

"Why not, Juno? Why should Jupiter stand in awe of thy face, Juno?" Ovid (Jupiter) replied.

"Because it is thy wife's face, Jupiter," Julia (Juno) answered.

Ovid (Jupiter) said, "What! Shall a husband be afraid of his wife's face? Will she paint it with makeup so horribly? We are a King, you cotquean — you scolding woman — and we will reign in our pleasures; and we will cudgel thee to death if thou find fault with us."

Jupiter sometimes threatened his wife with violence.

Julia (Juno) said:

"I will find fault with thee, King cuckold-maker."

A horny god, Jupiter made many husbands cuckolds.

Julia (Juno) continued:

"What! Shall the King of gods turn into the King of good fellows, and have no fellow in wickedness? This makes our poets, who know our profaneness, live as profane as we. By my godhead, Jupiter, I will join with all the other gods here, bind thee hand and foot, throw thee down into earth, and make a poor poet of thee, if thou abuse me thus."

Juno and some other gods and goddesses once attempted to bind Jupiter, but the sea-nymph Thetis rescued him.

"A right smart-tongued goddess; a right Juno," Gallus (Phoebus Apollo) said.

A right Juno is a true Juno. Juno was known for her jealousy, and Julia was being jealous.

"Juno, we will cudgel thee, Juno," Ovid (Jupiter) said. "We told thee so yesterday, when thou were jealous of us because of Thetis."

Thetis was a sea-nymph and the mother of Achilles, the greatest warrior of the Trojan War. Jupiter desired Thetis, but when he learned of a prophecy that she would give birth to a son who would be greater than his father, he decided to have her marry a mortal.

The Pyrgus (Ganymede) said to Ovid (Jupiter), "Today she had me in inquisition, too."

Apparently, Julia, like Juno, was jealous and had questioned the Pyrgus about any other women Ovid showed interest in.

Tucca (Mars) said to the Pyrgus (Ganymede), "Well said, my fine Phrygian fry; inform, inform."

Ganymede's father was the King of Phrygia in Asia Minor (roughly, modern Turkey).

Tucca was OK with the Pyrgus informing Ovid about the questioning.

Tucca (Mars) said to Crispinus (Mercury), "Give me some wine, King of heralds, so I may drink to my cockatrice."

Refusing wine from the Pryrus (Ganymede), Ovid (Jupiter) said, "No more, Ganymede."

He then said to Julia (Juno), "We will cudgel thee, Juno; by Styx, we will."

When a god swore by the Styx River, he was making an inviolable oath.

Julia (Juno) replied, "Aye, it is well; gods may grow impudent in iniquity, and they must not be told of it —"

Ovid (Jupiter) said, "Yea, we will knock our chin against our breast and shake thee out of Olympus into an oyster boat for thy scolding."

Oyster wives — women who sold oysters — were known for having loud voices.

Gods sometimes nodded the head while making a vow.

When Jupiter made an inviolable vow to Thetis to make the Trojans victorious for a while in Homer's *Iliad*, he nodded his head.

Julia (Juno) said:

"Your nose is not long enough to do it, Jupiter, even if all thy strumpets thou have among the stars took thy part."

Ovid's name is Publius Ovidius Naso. "Naso" means "large-nosed."

"Nose" sometimes meant "penis."

She continued:

"And there is never a star in thy forehead but shall be a horn, if thou persist in abusing me."

The horns would be the invisible horns of a cuckold.

To get revenge on Jupiter's sleeping with other women, Juno would sleep with other men.

Some of the women Jupiter slept with became stars, such as Maia, the leader of the Pleiades. Jupiter and Maia were the parents of Mercury.

Some of Jupiter's children by women other than Juno also became stars or constellations. For example, Castor and Pollux, sons of Jupiter and Leda; and Hercules, son of Jupiter and Alcmena.

"A good jest, indeed," Crispinus (Mercury) said.

Ovid (Jupiter) said, "We tell thee thou anger us, cotquean; and we will thunder thee in pieces for thy cotqueanity."

"Another good jest," Crispinus (Mercury) said.

Julia (Juno) may have held up two fingers, symbolizing the horns of a cuckold.

Albius (Vulcan) said, "O my hammers and my Cyclops! This boy Ganymede does not fill cups with enough wine to make us kind to one another."

Cyclops are one-eyed giants who help Vulcan forge thunderbolts for Jupiter.

Tucca (Mars) said to Albius (Vulcan), "Nor have thou collied — blackened — thy face enough, stinkard."

Taking a wine container, Albius (Vulcan) said, "I'll ply the table with nectar, and make them friends."

"Heaven is likely to have only a lame skinker, then," Hermogenes (Momus) said.

A skinker is a person who serves drinks.

Vulcan was born lame.

Albius (Vulcan) said:

"Wine and good livers make true lovers."

The liver was thought to be the seat of passion.

"Good livers" can also mean people who live well.

He continued:

"I'll sentence them together."

Pouring wine for Ovid and Julia, he said:

"Here, father; here, mother; for shame, drink yourselves drunk and forget this dissension. You two should cling together before our faces and give us an example of unity."

Albius (Vulcan) went around the table pouring wine.

"Oh, excellently spoken, Vulcan, suddenly!" Gallus (Phoebus Apollo) said.

"Jupiter may do well to prefer — promote — his tongue to some official position for his eloquence," Tibullus (Bacchus) said about Albius (Vulcan).

"His tongue shall be gent'man usher to his wit, and always go before it," Tucca (Mars) said.

In other words: Albius (Vulcan) will always speak before he thinks.

"An excellent fit office!" Albius (Vulcan) said.

"Aye, and an excellent good jest, besides," Crispinus (Mercury) said.

Hermogenes (Momus) said to Tucca (Mars), "What, have you hired Mercury to cry and proclaim your jests you make?"

"Momus, you are envious," Ovid (Vulcan) said.

Tucca (Mars) said to Hermogenes (Momus), "Why, you whoreson blockhead, it is your only block of wit in fashion, nowadays, to applaud other folks' jests."

A blockhead was a piece of wood used to shape hats.

Hermogenes (Momus) said to Tucca (Mars), "True — with those who are not artificers — creators — of jests themselves."

Hermogenes (Momus) said to Albius (Vulcan), "Vulcan, you nod; and the mirth of the feast droops."

"He has filled nectar so long that his brain swims in it," the Pyrgus (Ganymede) said.

Albius (Vulcan) was drunk from breathing in the fumes of the wine.

"What, do we nod, fellow gods?" Gallus (Phoebus Apollo) said. "Let music sound, and let us startle — rouse — our spirits with a song."

"Do, Apollo; thou are a good musician," Tucca (Mars) said to Gallus (Phoebus Apollo).

"What does Jupiter say?" Gallus (Phoebus Apollo) asked.

"Huh? Huh?" Ovid (Jupiter) said.

He was one of the ones who were nodding off and so had not been paying attention.

"Shall we have a song?" Gallus (Phoebus Apollo) asked.

"Why, do, do, sing," Ovid (Jupiter) said.

"Bacchus, what do you say?" Plautia (Ceres) asked.

"Ceres?" Tibullus (Bacchus) said to Plautia (Ceres).

Tibullus (Bacchus) had also been nodding off and not paying attention.

"But what do you say to this song?" Plautia (Ceres) asked.

"Sing, as far as I'm concerned," Tibullus (Bacchus) answered.

"Your belly weighs down your head, Bacchus," Julia (Juno) said. "Here's a song toward — imminent."

Tibullus (Bacchus) said, "Begin, Vulcan —"

"What else? What else?" Albius (Vulcan) replied.

Tucca (Mars) said, "Say, Jupiter —"

Ovid (Jupiter) said, "Mercury —"

Crispinus (Mercury) said, "Aye, say, say —"

Albius (Vulcan) began the song, and others joined in:

"Wake, our mirth begins to die.

"Quicken [Enliven] it with tunes and wine;
"Raise your notes; you're out. Fie, fie, [Bah, bah,]
"This drowsiness is an ill sign.
"We banish him [from] the choir [company] of gods
"That [Who] droops [and nods] again;
"Then all are men,
"For here's not one but nods."

No one present could be gods, for all were drowsy and nodding.

Ovid (Jupiter) said:

"I don't like this sudden and general heaviness — sleepiness — among our godheads; it is somewhat ominous.

"Apollo, command for us louder music, and let Mercury and Momus contend to please and revive our senses."

Hermogenes (Momus) sang:

"Then in a free and lofty strain
"Our broken tunes we thus repair;"

Crispinus (Mercury) sang:

"And we answer them again,
"Running division [Singing musical embellishments] on the panting air,"

Both Hermogenes and Crispinus sang:

"To celebrate this feast of sense
"As free from scandal as offence."

Hermogenes (Momus) sang:

"Here is beauty for the eye;"

Crispinus (Mercury) sang:

"For the ear, sweet melody;"

Hermogenes (Momus) sang:

"Ambrosiac odors for the smell;"

Crispinus (Mercury) sang:

"Delicious nectar for the taste;"

Both Hermogenes and Crispinus sang:

"For the touch, a lady's waist,
"Which doth [does] all the rest excel!"

Ovid (Jupiter) said:

"Aye; this has awakened us."

He then said to Crispinus (Mercury), "Mercury, our herald, go from ourself, the great god Jupiter, to the great emperor, Augustus Caesar; and command him from us (of whose bounty he has received his surname, Augustus) that for a thank-offering to our beneficence he presently sacrifice as a dish to this banquet his beautiful and wanton daughter Julia. She's a curst quean — a shrewish strumpet — tell him, and plays the scold behind his back; therefore, let her be sacrificed."

The sacrifice could be a sexual sacrifice.

He continued:

"Command him this, Mercury, in our high name of Jupiter *Altitonans*: Jupiter who thunders from on high."

Julia (Juno) said:

"Wait, feather-footed Mercury, and tell Augustus from us, the great Juno Saturnia: daughter of Saturn —"

Mercury's sandals had feathered wings.

She continued:

"— that if he thinks it hard to do as Jupiter has commanded him and sacrifice his daughter, that he had better to do so ten times than suffer her to love the well-nosed poet Ovid — whom he shall do well to whip, or cause to be whipped, about the Capitol, for soothing — encouraging — her in her follies."

The Capitol is the Capitoline Hill.

— 4.6 —

Augustus Caesar, Maecenas, Horace, Lupus, Histrio, and Minos entered the scene. Minos was guarded by some Lictors.

Looking at the revelers, his daughter Julia among them, Augustus Caesar said:

"What sight is this? Maecenas! Horace!"

Using the majestic plural, he said:

"Tell me, do we have our senses? Do we hear and see? Or are these just imaginary objects drawn by our imagination?"

He said to Maecenas and Horace:

"Why don't you speak?"

He had heard some of the revelers' conversation and now repeated:

"'Let us do sacrifice'?"

He continued:

"Are they the gods?

"Reverence, amazement, and fury fight in me."

The banqueters knelt before him.

Augustus Caesar continued:

"What? Do they kneel? Nay, then I see that what I thought impossible is true. Oh, impious sight!"

He turned his face away and said:

"Let me divert my eyes; the very thought everts — sets upside down — my soul with passion. Don't look, man. There is a panther, whose unnatural eye will strike thee dead."

The man was Augustus himself, and the panther was Julia.

Turning towards his daughter Julia, he said to himself:

"Turn, then, and die on her with her own death!"

He moved as if he would kill his daughter, fighting her as if she were an enemy whom he would kill even if it meant his own death.

Maecenas and Horace put themselves between Augustus Caesar and Julia and said, "What does imperial Caesar intend to do?"

Augustus Caesar said to Maecenas and Horace:

"What, would you have me let the strumpet live who for this pageant earns so many deaths?"

Tucca said quietly to the Pyrgus, "Boy, slink, boy."

He wanted to make an escape.

The Pyrgus said quietly to Tucca, "I pray to Jupiter that we are not followed by the scent, Master."

They smelled strongly of wine.

Tucca and the Pyrgus exited without calling attention to themselves.

Augustus Caesar asked Albius, "Tell me, sir, who are you?"

"I play Vulcan, sir," Albius said.

"But who are you, sir?" Augustus Caesar asked.

"Your citizen and jeweler, sir," Albius said.

Augustus Caesar said to Chloe, "And who are you, dame?"

The word "dame" was not used for upper-class women.

"I play Venus, forsooth," Chloe said.

The word "forsooth" was not used by upper-class women.

Augustus Caesar said, "I ask not who you play, but who you are?"

"Your citizen and a jeweler's wife, sir," Chloe answered.

Augustus Caesar asked Crispinus, "And you, good sir?"

"Your gentleman parcel-poet, sir," Crispinus answered.

A parcel-poet is a part-poet: a sort of poet.

"Oh, that profaned name!" Augustus Caesar said.

The name of "poet" was profaned by parcel-poets such as Crispinus.

Augustus Caesar said to Julia:

"And are these seemly — fit — company for thee, thou degenerate monster?"

He said to Horace and Maecenas:

"All the rest I know, and I hate all my knowledge of them because of their hateful sakes."

He hated the drunken poets before him whom he had caught in the presence of his daughter Julia.

Augustus Caesar said to Ovid, Gallus, and Tibullus:

"Are you, who first the deities inspired with skill of their high natures and their powers, the first abusers of their useful light, profaning thus their dignities in their forms, and making them like you, only counterfeits?"

Augustus Caesar distrusted theater, regarding it as only counterfeit and not real. He also regarded these poets as not real poets and not capable of writing correctly about the gods, whom they profane instead of praise, although the gods had given them poetic inspiration.

He continued:

"Oh, who shall follow virtue and embrace her, when her false bosom is found to be nothing but air? And yet from those embraces Centaurs spring who war with human peace and poison men."

Embracing false virtue creates bad things, as did Ixion, who embraced a counterfeit Juno.

Ixion, the King of the Lapiths, tried to rape Juno. Jupiter made a cloud in the shape of Juno. Ixion coupled with it, and from this union came Imbros, aka Centaurus, who mated with mares and created the Centaurs, most of whom were wild.

The Centaurs did such things as try to rape Hippodamia and the female guests at her wedding to King Pirithous of the Lapiths. Theseus (Pirithous' best friend) and other men were able to defeat the Centaurs in a battle that came to be known as the Centauromachy.

Augustus Caesar continued:

"Who shall with greater comforts — solace — comprehend virtue's unseen being and her excellence, when you, who teach and should eternize her, live as if she were no law to your lives, nor lived herself except with your idle breaths?"

In other words: Virtue is real, and the poets should teach others about her, but you counterfeit poets treat virtue as if she exists only in your idle words: You live as if virtue isn't real. How then can anyone take comfort in understanding virtue?

Using the majestic plural, Augustus Caesar continued:

"If you think gods but feigned, and virtue painted, know that we sustain an actual residence."

In other words: Maybe you counterfeit poets don't believe in gods and virtue, but let me tell you that I have a real residence.

Augustus Caesar continued:

"And with the title of an Emperor I retain an Emperor's spirit and imperial power, by which —"

He turned to Ovid and continued:

"— in imposition too remiss, licentious and lascivious Naso, for thy violent wrong in soothing the declined affections — the degraded and perverse inclinations — of our base daughter — we exile thy feet from all approach to our imperial court, on pain of death.

"Thy misbegotten love — Julia — we commit to the patronage of iron doors, since her soft-hearted sire cannot contain — control — her."

In other words: Julia will be guarded behind closed doors.

"Oh, my good lord, forgive her," Maecenas said. "Be like the gods."

"Let royal bounty, Caesar, mediate," Horace said.

Augustus Caesar said:

"There is no bounty to be shown to such people who have no real or royal goodness.

"Bounty is a spice — a species — of virtue; and what virtuous act can take effect on them who have no power of equal habitude — moral disposition — to apprehend and understand it, but live in worship of that idol, vice, as if there were no virtue except shape — something unreal — that is imposed by strong imagination?

"This shows that their knowledge is mere ignorance.

"This shows that their far-fetched dignity of soul is a fancy.

"And this shows that all their solemn pretension to gravity is a mere vainglory."

He said to the Lictors:

"Hence, away with them. Take them away from here."

The Lictors placed Ovid and Julia under separate guard and began to clear the room of banqueters.

Augustus Caesar then said:

"I will prefer to know no one but such as rule their lives by knowledge, including knowledge of virtue, and can becalm all the sea of humors — whims and fancies — with the marble trident of their strong spirits.

"Others fight below

"With gnats and shadows; others nothing know."

In the Land of the Dead, some souls — shadows — of soldiers exist. When Aeneas visited the Land of the Dead in the *Aeneid*, the shadows of Greek soldiers tried to utter war cries, but they could manage only feeble whispers. When Odysseus visited the Land of the Dead in the *Odyssey*, the shadows,

except for the prophet Tiresias, knew nothing — not even who they are —
until they drank some of the blood from the sacrifice that Odysseus made for
them.

Tucca, Crispinus, and the Pyrgus talked together.

Tucca said to Crispinus, "What's become of my little punk: Venus? And the poltfoot stinkard, her husband, huh?"

"Poltfoot" means club-footed and refers to the lame blacksmith god, Vulcan, whom Albius played in the masquerade. Venus, of course, is Chloe.

"Oh, they have ridden home in the coach as fast as the wheels can run," the Pyrgus said.

Tucca said:

"God Jupiter is banished, I hear, and his cockatrice, Juno, locked up. By God's heart, if all the poetry in Parnassus should get me to be an actor again, I'll sell the other actors my share for a sesterce — a very small amount.

"But this is Humors, Horace, that goat-footed envious slave!"

"Goat-footed" refers to satyrs and satirists. A satyr is a half-human, half-goat nature spirit who loves wine, women, and song.

Ben Jonson wrote plays about humors, and Tucca gave Horace (and Ben Jonson) that name now.

Humors can be defining personal characteristics. Horace's main humor is being a poet.

Tucca continued:

"He's turned into a fawner now, a toady, an informer, the rogue; it is he who has betrayed us all. Didn't you see him with the Emperor, crouching?"

According to Tucca, Horace toadies up to Augustus Caesar.

"Yes," Crispinus said.

Tucca said:

"Well, follow me. Thou shall libel and I'll cudgel the rascal."

He said to the Pyrgus:

"Boy, provide me a truncheon — a club."

Tucca then said to both the Pyrgus and Crispinus:

"Revenge shall 'gratulate' him, *tam Marti, quam Mercurio*."

"Gratulate him" means 1) welcome him, and 2) thank him.

The Latin means "as much for Mars as for Mercury."

Tucca played Mars in the masquerade, and Crispinus played Mercury. Tucca had been threatening to beat Horace, and Crispinus intended to slander Horace, thereby stealing his good name. Mars is the god of war, and Mercury is the god of thieves.

The Pyrgus said, "Aye, but master, take heed how you let this be known; Horace is a man of the sword."

Ben Jonson once killed a fellow actor in a duel.

"That is true, indeed; they say he's valiant," Crispinus said.

"Valiant?" Tucca said. "So is my arse. Gods and fiends! I'll blow him into air when I meet him next. He dares not fight with a puckfist: a puffball mushroom."

"Master, here he comes," the Pyrgus said.

Horace walked near them.

Tucca asked:

"Where?"

Seeing Horace, he said politely to him:

"Jupiter save thee, my good poet, my noble prophet."

Then he added under his beath:

"My little fat Horace!"

Tucca then said quietly to Crispinus and the Pyrgus:

"I scorn to beat the rogue in the court, and I saluted him thus politely so that he would not suspect anything, the rascal."

Fighting within the court was illegal.

He added:

"Come, we'll go see how forward our journeyman is toward the untrussing of him."

A journeyman craftsman can be hired by the day. Demetrius was the journeyman.

"Untrussing" meant undressing; the plotters were planning to "expose" Horace.

"Do you hear me, Captain?" Crispinus said. "I'll write nothing in it but what is innocent and harmless, because I want to be able to swear that I am innocent."

Tucca, Crispinus, and the Pyrgus exited. Horace was still present.

Maecenas entered the scene. From another door arrived Lupus, with the Lictors and Histrio.

Horace said to Lupus, "So, why don't you pursue the Emperor for your reward now, Lupus?"

Lupus, suspecting treason, was the person who had brought Augustus Caesar to the masquerade at which Caesar banished Ovid and Julia.

Maecenas said to Asinius Lupus, who had started to leave:

"Wait, Asinius. Wait, you and your stager — actor —and your band of Lictors.

"I hope your service merits more respect than thus, without a thanks, to be sent away from here!"

"Well, well, jest on, jest on," Histrio said.

Horace said to Histrio, "Thou base, unworthy groom —"

A groom is a serving-man.

"Aye, aye, it is good," Lupus said sarcastically.

Horace said to Lupus:

"Was this the treason? Was this the dangerous plot thy clamorous tongue so bellowed through the court? Had thou no other project to increase thy grace with Caesar but this wolfish train, to prey upon the life of innocent mirth and harmless pleasures, bred of noble wit?"

The name "Lupus" means "wolf" in Latin.

The word "train" can mean 1) scheme, and/or 2) group of followers.

Horace continued:

"Go away! I loathe thy presence!

"Those who are such as thou are the moths and scarabs — dung beetles — of a state, the bane of empires, and the dregs of courts, who, to endear themselves to any employment, don't care whose fame they blast, whose life they endanger.

"And under a disguised and cobweb — flimsy — mask of love for their sovereign, they vomit forth their own prodigious malice; and pretending to be the props and columns of his safety, the guard to his person and his peace, they disturb it most with their false lapwing cries."

Lapwings are birds that nest on the ground, and they are loudest when away from their nest to keep enemies away from their nestlings. Sometimes they pretend to have an injured wing and cry while leading enemies away from the nest. When the enemy is a safe distance from the nest, the lapwing takes flight. A group of lapwings is called a deceit of lapwings.

"Good. Caesar shall know of this, believe it," Lupus said.

Lupus, Histrio, and the Lictors exited.

Maecenas said:

"Caesar does know it, wolf, and in accordance with his knowledge he will, I hope, reward your base endeavors.

"Princes who will but hear or give access to such officious spies can never be safe:

"They take in poison with an open ear,

"And, free from danger, become slaves to fear."

Some poisons, including poisonous words, are poured into the victim's ear.

Alone, Ovid mourned being separated from Julia by her father. He said to himself:

"Banished from the court? Let me be banished from life, since the chief end of life is there concluded and confined."

Ovid's relationship with Julia was concluded — ended — with her confinement to her chamber.

Ovid continued:

"Within the court is all the kingdom bounded and contained, and as her sacred sphere does comprehend ten thousand times so much as so much place in any other part of all the empire, so everybody moving in her sphere contains ten thousand times as much in him as any other her choice orb excludes."

According to Ptolemaic astronomy, the Sun and the planets were fixed in spheres that moved around the Earth, which was the center of the universe.

According to Ovid, the court was a sphere in which was that which was ten thousand times more valuable than any other sphere in the empire. Anyone moving within the court's orbit had ten thousand times as much in him as any other man whom the court's sphere excluded.

Julia, however, was in the court, and the pronoun "her" encompassed Julia in addition to the court.

Ovid continued:

"As in a circle a magician then is safe against the spirit he excites, but out of it the magician is subject to his rage and loses all the virtue of his art, so I, exiled from the circle of the court, lose all the good gifts that in it I enjoyed."

Magicians would draw a circle in which they would stand to be safe from any evil demon they called up.

Some circles are vaginas, and some stands are erections.

Ovid continued:

"No virtue is current, except with her stamp, and no vice is vicious, but is blanched with her white hand."

Current coinage is legal coinage with the sovereign's — Queen Elizabeth I's — stamp of approval.

Ovid continued:

"The court is the abstract — the epitome — of all Rome's desert and merit, and my dear Julia is the abstract — the epitome — of the court.

"I think, now I come near her, I respire — breathe in — some air of that recent comfort I received, and while the evening with her modest veil — the dusk of evening — gives leave to such poor shadows — ghosts — as myself to steal abroad, I, like a heartless ghost, without the living body of my love will here walk and attend her."

Ovid had received comfort from Julia: a note saying where she was imprisoned.

Ovid continued:

"For I know that she is imprisoned not far from here, and she hopes to bribe her strict guardian to allow her so much admittance as to speak to me and cheer my fainting spirits with her breath."

In Julia's note, she had written that she hoped to be able to bribe her guardian so that she could speak to him.

Julia appeared at the window of her chamber.

"Ovid? My love?" she said.

"Here, heavenly Julia," Ovid said.

Julia said:

"Here and not here!"

Ovid was here, but he was banished. And he was here, but he was below and he was not standing by her.

Julia continued:

"Oh, how that word 'here' plays with both our fortunes, differing like our selves: Both one, and yet divided as if we were opposed to each other as enemies!

"I high, thou low! Oh, this our plight of place doubly presents the two lets — hindrances — of our love, local and ceremonial height and lowness; in both ways I am too high and thou are too low."

The two hindrances of their love were height and lowness. Julia was high in her chamber, and Ovid was low on the ground; in addition, Julia's social position was higher than Ovid's.

"Local" referred to location, and "ceremonial" referred to society.

Julia continued:

"Our minds are even, yet; oh, why should our bodies, which are their slaves, be so without their rule?"

In other words: Our minds are equal, so why shouldn't our bodies be ruled by the same principle of equality?

Julia continued:

"I'll cast myself down to thee; if I die, I'll forever live with thee. No height of birth, of social position, of duty, or of cruel power shall keep me from thee.

"Even if my father would lock this body up within a tomb of brass, yet I'll be with thee.

"If the forms of love I hold now in my soul be made one substance with it, if that soul is immortal, and if it is the same as it is now, then death cannot raze the affects — the desire — she now retains — and then she may be anywhere she will."

Plato believed in Forms. The Forms are the highest form of reality, and they are eternal and unchanging. Plato believed that there were many Forms. There is a Form for Tree, of which individual physical trees are only images. There is also a Form for Human Being and Forms for other physical objects. In addition, there are Forms for Beauty, Truth, Justice, Excellence, Piety, etc.

Julia was saying that in her soul was the Form for Love. Both the Form of Love and her soul were immortal, and if the two were united, then her death would not erase knowledge of that Form of Love.

The phrase "forms of love" with a lower-case 'f' means manifestations of the Form of Love. One such manifestation was her love for Ovid, which participated in the Form of Love.

In other words: She loved Ovid now, and since her soul was immortal and Love was immortal, she would continue to love him after death.

Julia continued:

"The souls of parents do not rule children's souls when death sets both in their dissolved estates — when death separates the soul and body of the child and of each parent — then there is no child, nor father; and then eternity frees all from any temporal respect and obedience due to parents.

"I come, my Ovid; take me in thine arms and let me breathe my soul into thy breast!"

She made a movement as if to throw herself down.

Ovid said:

"Oh, stay, my love! The hopes thou conceive of thy quick — swift and living — death and of thy future life are not authentic and valid.

"Thou choose death so thou might enjoy thy love in the other life.

"But know, my princely love, when thou are dead thou only must survive in perfect and unalloyed soul; and in the soul are no affections."

Affections are passions and desires, including sexual desires.

Ovid continued:

"We pour out our affections with our blood, and with our blood's affections fade our loves.

"No life has love in such sweet state as this.

"No essence is so dear to moody sense as flesh and blood, whose quintessence — innermost nature — is sense.

"Beauty composed of blood and flesh moves more and is more plausible — acceptable, agreeable, pleasing — to blood and flesh than spiritual beauty can be to the spirit.

"Such apprehension — perception — as we have in dreams when sleep, the bond of senses, locks them up, such shall we have when death destroys them quite.

"If love is then thy object, exchange not life for death. Live high and happy still; I, still below, close with my fortunes, in thy height shall enjoy."

Ovid will be "close" — that is, hidden away — because of his banishment. In addition he will be "close" — near to — his low fortune. But he will still rejoice that Julia is alive.

Julia said:

"Woe is me, that virtue, whose brave eagle's wings with every stroke blow stars in burning heaven, should like a swallow preying toward storms fly close to earth, and with an eager plume — fierce flight — pursue those objects that none else can see, but seem to all the world the empty air."

In other words: In our case, virtue is like an eagle that flies close to the earth (like a swallow flying into the winds of a storm as it hunts) and pursues sustenance that no one can see.

Because Ovid and Julia are separated, their love lacks sustenance. The two cannot fly high, as they would in a world in which her father did not oppose their love.

Julia continued:

"Thus thou, poor Ovid, and all virtuous men must prey like swallows on invisible food, pursuing flies, or nothing; and thus love and every worldly fancy is transposed and transformed by worldly tyranny into whatever plight — peril — it wishes."

She then addressed her father, who was not present, in an apostrophe:

"O father, since thou did not give me my mind, don't strive to rule it; take only what thou gave me — my body — into thy control. Thy affections and inclinations don't rule me. I must bear all my griefs. Let me use and enjoy all my pleasures. Virtuous love was never scandal to a goddess' state."

Julia had acted the role of Juno, but her doing so was not scandalous.

Julia then said:

"But my father is inflexible! And, my dear love, Ovid, thy life may perhaps be shortened by the length of my unwilling speeches to depart.

"Farewell, sweet life. Even though thou, Ovid, are yet exiled from the officious — interfering — court, enjoy me amply still.

"My soul in this my breath enters thine ears, and on this turret's floor I will lie dead until we may meet again."

She knelt and said:

"In this proud height I kneel beneath thee in my prostrate love and kiss the happy sands that kiss thy feet."

She kissed the literal floor of the turret and the metaphorical happy sands on which Ovid stood, and then she rose.

Julia continued:

"Great Jove submits — reduces — a scepter to a cell, and lovers, rather than part, will meet in hell."

Julia's high birth had turned into a prison cell for her. Nevertheless, Julia's love for Ovid was stronger than her father's power over her. She would not stop loving Ovid.

Ovid said:

"Farewell, all company, and if I could, all light, with thee! Hell's shade should hide my brows until thy dear beauty's beams redeemed my vows."

He would commit suicide if he were capable of it.

Ovid started to leave.

Julia called him back:

"Ovid, my love! Alas, may we not stay a little longer, do thou think, undiscerned?"

Turning back, Ovid said:

"For thine own good, fair goddess, do not stay.

"Who would engage — put at risk — a firmament of fires shining in thee, for me, a fallen star?

"Be gone, sweet life-blood. If I should discern thyself but touched for my sake, I should die."

Julia could be touched in a way that would hurt her, and Ovid would literally die.

But "to die" can mean "to have an orgasm," and if Ovid could touch Julia, he would figuratively die.

Julia said, "I will be gone, then, and not heaven itself shall draw me back."
She started to leave.

Ovid said, "Yet, Julia, if thou will, a little longer stay."

Julia returned and said, "I am content to stay a little longer."

Ovid said, "O mighty Ovid! What the sway of heaven could not retire — draw back — my breath has turned back."

"Who shall leave first, my love?" Julia said. "My passionate — sorrowful — eyes will not endure seeing thee turn from me."

"If thou go first, my soul will follow thee," Ovid said.

"Then we must stay," Julia said.

Ovid said:

"Woe is me, there is no stay in amorous pleasures."

The word "no stay" meant 1) no permanence, and 2) no stopping.

Ovid continued:

"If both stay, both die."

If both stay and are caught by Julia's father, both will die.

But the word "die" in Elizabethan times also meant "have an orgasm," and so the words also mean, If both of us stay and have sex, both of us will have orgasms.

Ovid said:

"I hear thy father — hence, my deity!"

Julia exited.

Alone, Ovid said to himself:

"Fear forges sounds in my deluded ears. I did not hear thy father; I am mad with love.

"There is no spirit under heaven that works with such illusion; yet let such witchcraft kill me, before a sound mind without it save my life!"

He preferred to die while mad with love rather than live without love.

Ovid knelt and said:

"Here, on my knees, I worship the blest place that held my goddess, and the loving air that enclosed her body in its silken arms.

"Vain Ovid! Kneel not to the place nor air. She's in thy heart."

Ovid rose and said:

"Rise, then, and worship there.

The truest wisdom silly men can have is dotage on the follies of their flesh."

The word "silly" meant "deserving of sympathy and compassion."

CHAPTER 5
— 5.1 —

Augustus Caesar was sitting on his throne. With him, standing, were Gallus, Tibullus, Maecenas, and Horace.

Using the majestic plural, Augustus Caesar pardoned Gallus and Tibullus:

"We who have conquered always to spare the conquered, and we who have loved to make inflictions feared, not felt, have grieved to reprove and was joyful to reward, and have been more proud of reconcilement than revenge, say this:

"Return again into the recent state of our love and respect, worthy Cornelius Gallus and Tibullus.

"You both are gentlemen.

"You, Cornelius, are a soldier of renown and the first Provost who ever let our Roman eagles fly on swarthy Egypt, quarried with her spoils."

Elevated by Augustus Caesar from humble origins, Gallus had led the Roman army into Egypt and had become the country's first Provost, or ruling overseer.

Hunting hawks were rewarded with part of the prey — quarry — after a successful hunt. Rome was rewarded with Egyptian riches.

Eagles were the insignia on Roman standards.

The people of Egypt were swarthy: of dark complexion.

Augustus Caesar continued:

"Yet, not to bear cold forms nor men's outer conditions without the inward fires and lives of men, you both have virtues shining through your shapes to show your titles are not written on posts or hollow statues — the best men without Promethean stuffings reached from heaven are nothing but posts and hollow statues."

Prometheus gave divine sparks to Humankind.

In mythology, Prometheus created Humankind from clay and breathed life into Humankind. He also stole fire from the gods and gave it to Humankind.

A man — even the best man (best in appearance and social status) — without those Promethean divine sparks is like a post or a hollow statue.

The Promethean divine sparks are virtues.

Augustus Caesar continued:

Gallus and Tibullus have inward virtues that shine outward so that Humankind can see them.

"Sweet poesy's sacred garlands crown your gentry. Poesy is, of all the faculties — abilities — on Earth, the most abstract and perfect, if she is true born and nursed with all the sciences — branches of knowledge.

"She can so mold Rome and her monuments within the liquid marble of her lines that they shall stand fresh and miraculous even when they mix with innovating — changing — dust."

The oxymoron "liquid marble" refers to flowing lines of eternal poetry. Even after the Roman Coliseum is a literal ruin, Rome's poetry — such as Virgil's *Aeneid,* in which Aeneas, a surviving Trojan, becomes an important ancestor of the Roman people — shall stand fresh and miraculous and keep Rome and the Roman Coliseum fresh and miraculous.

Augustus Caesar continued:

"In poetry's sweet streams shall our brave Roman spirits chase and swim after death, with their choice deeds shining on their white shoulders; and therein shall Tiber and our famous rivers fall with such attraction that the ambitious — closely encircling — line of the round world shall to her center shrink to hear their music; and for these high qualities Caesar shall reverence the Pierian arts."

In other words:

Poetry shall make Rome and the Roman people remembered, as indeed do Virgil's *Aeneid* and the works of Horace.

The entire world shall come to its center — Rome — either literally or figuratively to hear the music of its poetry.

The Muses lived in Pieria and frolicked by its streams.

Maecenas said:

"Your Majesty's high grace to poesy shall stand against all the dull detractions of leaden souls, who, for the vain assumings — pretensions — of some, quite worthless of her sovereign wreaths, contain — regard — her worthiest prophets in contempt."

In other words: Augustus Caesar's appreciation of true poetry will be a bulwark against bad poets who denigrate true poets.

Gallus said:

"Happy is Rome of all earth's other states, to have so true and great a president — governor and precedent, aka model — for her inferior spirits to imitate as Caesar is, who adds to the Sun influence and luster, in increasing thus his inspirations, kindling fire in us."

In other words: Augustus Caesar honors Phoebus Apollo, the Sun-god and the god of poetry, by praising poetry. Caesar is also a good model for Roman citizens to imitate.

Horace said:

"Phoebus Apollo himself shall kneel at Caesar's shrine and deck it with bay garlands dewed with wine to reward the worship Caesar does to him."

In other words: Apollo himself will reward Augustus Caesar with laurel wreaths for defending poetry.

Horace continued:

"Whereas other princes, hoisted to their thrones by Fortune's passionate and disordered power, sit in their height like clouds before the sun, hindering his — the sun's — comforts; and by their excess of cold in virtue and cross heat in vice, thunder and tempest on those learned heads whom Caesar with such honor does advance."

In other words, other princes who have been elevated by luck, not merit, block Apollo's gift of poetry to Humankind and storm against true poets such as those whom Augustus Caesar promotes and rewards. These bad princes are coldly indifferent to virtue and hotly in pursuit of sin.

Tibullus said:

"All human business Fortune does command without all order, and with her blind hand she, blind, bestows blind gifts that always have nursed they see not who nor how, but always the worst."

In other words: Tibullus believes that Lady Fortune is blind and hands out her gifts blindly and without order to bad people.

Using the third person, Augustus Caesar said:

"Caesar, as regards his rule and as regards whatever resources Lady Fortune puts in his hand, shall dispose it as if his hand had eyes and soul in it: with worth and judgment."

In other words: When Augustus Caesar gave gifts, he did so with open eyes: He would reward the deserving virtuous people, including poets.

Augustus Caesar continued:

"Hands that part with gifts either will restrain their use, without desert or with a misery — miserliness — numbed to virtue's right, work as if they had no soul to govern them, and quite reject her, severing their estates — condition of life, and material wealth — from human order.

"Whosoever can and will not cherish virtue is no man."

In other words: Hands that give gifts or withhold gifts without considering the virtue of those who receive or do not receive them are soulless and do not value virtue.

Some Roman equites — Knights — entered the scene.

The Knights were the social class immediately below the noble class.

"Virgil is now at hand, imperial Caesar," a Knight said.

"Rome's honor is at hand, then," Augustus Caesar said.

Virgil was and is the greatest Roman poet.

Augustus Caesar said to the Knights:

"Fetch a chair and set it on our right hand, the place of honor, where it is fitting that Rome's honor, and our own, should always sit."

The Knights set the chair in place; then they exited.

Augustus Caesar said, "Now that Virgil has come out of Campania in west central Italy, I don't doubt that he has finished all the books of his *Aeneid*, which like another soul I long to enjoy."

The *Aeneid* consists of 12 books, but if the *Aeneid* were written today, we would call them chapters.

Augustus Caesar said to Maecenas, Gallus, and Tibullus:

"What do you three think of Virgil, gentlemen, you who are of his profession, though ranked higher?"

Virgil was ranked higher critically, but his birth in the social order was lower. His father was a farmer, but a farmer with much land.

Augustus Caesar then said:

"Or, Horace, what do thou say, thou who are the poorest and likeliest to envy or to detract?"

Ben Jonson's father was a bricklayer.

The Roman Horace had inherited a small estate, but he had fought against Augustus Caesar and so had lost it. Augustus Caesar gave him amnesty.

In his reply, Horace pointed out that knowledge is more important than wealth:

"Caesar speaks in the manner of common men in this to make a difference of me for my poorness, as if the filth of poverty sunk as deep into a knowing spirit as the bane of riches does into an ignorant soul.

"No, Caesar, they are pathless, moorish — boggy — minds that, being once made rotten with the dung of damned riches, forever afterward sink beneath the steps of any villainy."

In other words: Ignorant souls, when poisoned by wealth, become pathless and the only imprints they receive are from the metaphorical steps of villainy.

Horace continued:

"But knowledge is the nectar that keeps sweet a perfect soul even in this grave of sin: the body, and society.

"And as for my soul, it is as free — unfettered by poverty and generous — as Caesar's, for what I know is due I'll give to all.

"He who detracts or envies virtuous merit

"Is always the covetous and the ignorant spirit."

Augustus Caesar replied:

"Thanks, Horace, for thy free and wholesome sharpness, which pleases Caesar more than servile fawnings.

"A flattered prince soon turns into the prince of fools, and for thy sake we'll put no difference more between the great and good for being poor.

"Tell us then, beloved Horace, thy true thought and opinion about Virgil."

Horace said:

"I judge him to be of a rectified — refined — spirit, by many revolutions of discourse in his bright reason's influence, refined from all the tartarous — unrefined — moods of common men.

"He bears the nature and similitude of a right heavenly body; he is most severe in fashion and collection — shaping and composing — of himself, and then as clear and confident as Jove."

Virgil's spirit is more refined than the spirits of common men. Virgil's spirit is in the heavens because of his bright reason, while the spirits of common men are tartarous.

Tartarus is the Underworld, especially the part where evil-doers are punished. The word "tartarous," however, is derived from tartarous acid, an early name for tartaric acid.

Gallus said, "And yet so chaste — pure — and tender is his ear in suffering any syllable to pass that he thinks may become the honored name of issue to his so examined self that all the lasting fruits of his full merit in his own poems he does still distaste, as if his mind's piece, which he strove to paint, could not with fleshly pencils have her right."

Virgil is very critical of his own work — even his best work.

In fact, the *Aeneid* was not quite completed at his death — a few lines are only half-lines. On his deathbed, Virgil requested that the manuscript be burned, but Augustus Caesar denied that request. The thought of the *Aeneid* being burned and not being passed down to us gives some classicists such as Elizabeth Vandiver nightmares.

Tibullus said:

"But to confirm that his works have sovereign worth, this observation, I think, more than serves, and is not common:

"That which he has written is with such judgment labored and distilled through all the necessary uses of our lives that, could a man remember but Virgil's lines, the man should not touch at any serious point but he might breathe Virgil's spirit out of him."

In other words: In his works, Virgil has written important passages about all serious subjects.

In the Middle Ages, people concerned about an important question or subject would open the *Aeneid* and point to a passage at random. Sometimes, the passage shed light on the answer to the question. Some people have done this with the Bible.

Augustus Caesar said, "You mean he might repeat part of his works, as fit for any conference — discussion and reasoning — he can use?"

In any conversation, a man could use quotations from Virgil's works and they would be fitting for the conversation. They would contribute to the conversation, not be a distraction.

"True, royal Caesar," Tibullus said.

"Worthily observed, and a most worthy virtue in his works," Augustus Caesar said.

He then said, "What does material — full of good sense — Horace think of Virgil's learning?"

Horace said:

"His learning does not labor the school-like gloss that most consists in echoing words and terms and soonest wins a man an empty name, nor does his learning labor any long or far-fetched circumstance wrapped in the curious generalities of arts.

"Instead, his learning has a direct and analytic sum of all the worth and first effects of arts."

In other words: Virgil's learning is not abstruse and overly difficult but instead it clearly reveals the worth and value of knowledge and skill.

Horace continued:

"And as for his poesy, it is so rammed — crammed — with life that it shall gather strength of life with being and live hereafter more admired than now."

In other words: Virgil's poetry is so good that it will become more admired in the future than now: It will become a classic.

Augustus Caesar said, "This one consent in all your dooms — judgments — of him, and mutual loves of all your individual merits, argues a truth of merit in you all."

Virgil entered the scene. Some Roman Knights escorted him.

"Look, here comes Virgil," Augustus Caesar said. "We will rise and greet him."

He stood up.

Augustus Caesar then said:

"Welcome to Caesar, Virgil. Caesar and Virgil shall differ but in sound; to Caesar, Virgil, because of his expressed greatness, shall be made a second surname; and to Virgil, Caesar shall be made a second surname."

Romans were given an additional name as an honor. For example, Publius Cornelius Scipio was given the name "Africanus" in honor of his defeat of Hannibal and Carthage in North Africa in the Second Punic War.

Augustus Caesar then said:

"Where are thy famous books of the *Aeneid*? Do us the grace to let us see them, and surfeit on their sight."

Virgil replied:

"Worthless they are of Caesar's gracious eyes if they were perfect.

"Much more are they worthless with their faults, which yet are more than my time could supply the remedy.

"And if great Caesar's expectation could be satisfied with any other service, I would not show them to him."

Virgil was saying that even if his verses were perfect, they would still not be worthy enough for Augustus Caesar to see them.

"Virgil is too modest or seeks in vain to make our longings more," Augustus Caesar said. "Show them, sweet Virgil."

Virgil replied, "Then, in such due fear as befits presenters of great works to Caesar, I humbly show them."

Augustus Caesar accepted the manuscript from Virgil and said:

"Let us now behold a human soul made visible in life, and more refulgent — radiant — in a senseless paper than in the sensual complement — ceremony — of Kings."

In other words: A paper containing words of true poetry reveals a human soul and makes it more radiant than does the sensuous, luxurious ceremony of Kings.

He returned the manuscript and said:

"Read, read it thyself, dear Virgil. Let me not profane one accent with an untuned tongue. Best matter, badly shown, shows worse than bad."

He indicated the chair on his right and said:

"See then this chair, on purpose set for thee to read thy poem in."

Virgil made a motion as if to refuse the seat.

Augustus Caesar said:

"Don't refuse it.

"Virtue without presumption place may take

"Above best kings, whom only she should make."

Virgil said:

"It will be thought a thing ridiculous to present eyes, and to all future times a gross untruth, that any poet, void of birth or wealth or temporal dignity, should with fitness and decorum transcend and surpass Caesar's chair.

"Poor virtue raised, high birth and wealth set under,

"Crosses heaven's courses and makes worldlings wonder."

Heaven's courses are the orbits or spheres of planets. According to Virgil, even a virtuous poet ought not to ascend higher than those of high birth and wealth.

Augustus Caesar said, "The course of heaven and fate itself in this will Caesar cross; much more all worldly custom."

He was willing to raise Virgil above high birth and wealth.

Horace said:

"Custom in course of honor ever errs,

"And they are best whom Fortune least prefers."

"In course of honor" means either "in pursuit of honor" or "in bestowing honor."

Augustus Caesar said:

"Horace has but more strictly spoken our thoughts. The vast, rude swinge — uneducated power — of general confluence — the common mob — is in particular ends exempt from sense, and therefore reason, which in right should be the special rector — ruler — of all harmony, shall show we are a man distinct by it from those whom custom enraptures in her press."

Augustus Caesar will be different from common people who follow conventional thought because he will follow reason rather than custom.

Caesar took and opened the manuscript of the *Aeneid* at random and said, "Ascend, then, Virgil, and, where first by chance we here have turned thy book, do thou first read."

Virgil said:

"Great Caesar has his will. I will do what he wishes and will ascend to the dais.

"It would be a simple injury to his free hand, which sweeps the cobwebs from unused virtue and makes her shine proportioned to her worth, to be more nice — more reluctant and unwilling — to entertain his grace than he is choice and liberal to afford it."

Virgil mounted his chair on the dais and prepared to read.

Augustus Caesar said to the Knights, "Gentlemen of our chamber, guard the doors and let none enter. Peace and silence."

He then said, "Begin, good Virgil."

Virgil began to read a passage from Book 4 of the *Aeneid*, which is about the love affair of Aeneas and Dido, the Queen of Carthage. In this passage, Aeneas and Dido consummate their love in a cave. Quickly, rumors of their love affair spread throughout Carthage and the surrounding territory.

Virgil read:

"Meanwhile the skies began to thunder, and in tail

"Of that, fell pouring storms of sleet and hail.

"The Tyrian lords and Trojan youth each where [everywhere],

"With Venus' Dardan nephew, now in fear

"Seek out for several [different, separate] shelter through the plain,

"Whilst floods come rolling from the hills amain [violently]."

The Tyrian lords are men from Tyre. Dido and the Carthaginians are from the Phoenician city of Tyre.

The Dardan — Trojan — nephew of Venus is Ascanius, Aeneas' son and Venus' grandson. The Latin word for "grandchild" is *nepos*. Elizabethan English gives a wide meaning to the word "nephew."

Virgil continued reading:

"*Dido a cave, the Trojan prince [Aeneas] the same*
"*Lighted upon [Alighted upon, aka discovered]. There Earth, and heaven's great dame*
"*That [Who] has the charge of marriage [Juno, goddess of marriage], first gave sign*
"*Unto this contract; fire and air did shine,*
"*As guilty of the match, and from the hill*
"*The nymphs with shriekings do the region fill.*
"*Here first began their bane. This day was ground*
"*Of all their ills. For now nor [neither] rumor's sound*
"*Nor nice respect of state moves Dido aught [at all];*
"*Her love no longer now by stealth is sought;*
"*She calls this wedlock, and with that fair name*
"*Covers her fault. Forthwith the bruit and fame [gossip and rumor]*
"*Through all the greatest Libyan towns is gone;*
"*Fame, a fleet evil, than which is swifter none,*
"*That moving grows and flying gathers strength,*
"*Little at first, and fearful, but at length*
"*She dares attempt the skies, and stalking proud*
"*With feet on ground, her head doth [does] pierce a cloud!*
"*This child our parent Earth, stirred up with spite*
"*Of all the gods, brought forth; and, as some write,*
"*She was last sister of that giant race*
"*That thought to scale Jove's court; right swift of pace*
"*And swifter far of wing; a monster vast*
"*And dreadful. Look how many plumes are placed*
"*On her huge corpse, so many waking eyes*
"*Stick underneath; and, which may stranger rise*
"*In the report, as many tongues she bears,*
"*As many mouths, as many list'ning ears.*
"*Nightly in midst of all the heaven she flies,*
"*And through the earth's dark shadow shrieking cries;*
"*Nor do her eyes once bend to taste sweet sleep.*
"*By day on tops of houses she doth [does] keep,*
"*Or on high towers, and doth [does] thence affright [frighten]*

"Cities and towns of most conspicuous site.

"As covetous she is of tales and lies

"As prodigal of truth. This monster [Rumor] ...."

Below is an excerpt from David Bruce's *Virgil's* Aeneid: *A Retelling in Prose* that retells the above passage.

"[...] a storm hurled hail at them. All scattered and sought shelter. Dido and Aeneas found and entered the same cave. Here the goddesses Earth and Juno lit what resembled wedding torches. Here nymphs sang what resembled a wedding song. Here the sky witnessed what resembled a wedding. But although Juno provided the trappings of a wedding, this was not a legal wedding. Aeneas did not hold the torch that a groom holds in a real marriage. Aeneas did not make the vows that a groom makes in a real marriage.

"Dido called her relationship with Aeneas a marriage, but it was really an affair. Dido used the word 'marriage' to lessen her feeling of guilt.

"Rumors of the affair spread quickly to all the cities of Libya. Evil moves quickly, and of all evils, rumor moves the quickest. Rumor is the daughter of Mother Earth, who bore her after Jupiter had killed two of her sons: the Titan Coeus and the Giant Enceladus. Mother Earth gave birth to Rumor as a way to get revenge for the death of these sons.

"Rumor has wings and many feathers. Her many eyes never sleep, and she has many tongues and many ears. By night she flies, and by day she watches and listens. She values lies as much as she values truths."

Virgil continued reading briefly as Lupus entered the scene, but Virgil's words were drowned out by noise.

Holding a paper, Lupus came through the door, meeting the Knights on guard. He was attended by some Lictors.

Tucca, Crispinus, Demetrius, and Aesop attempted to crowd in after Lupus.

Aesop was an actor.

"Come, follow me, assist me, second me!" Lupus said to Tucca, Crispinus, Demetrius, and Aesop.

He then asked the Knights, "Where's the Emperor?"

"Sir, you must pardon us," the First Knight said.

"Caesar is private now," the Second Knight said. "You may not enter."

"Not enter?" Tucca said.

He then said to Lucca, "Charge them upon their allegiance, cropshin."

A cropshin is an inferior herring.

"We have an order to the contrary, sir," the First Knight said.

"I pronounce you all traitors, horrible traitors!" Lupus said. "What! Do you know my affairs? I have matter of danger and state to impart to Caesar!"

"What noise is there?" Augustus Caesar asked. "Who's that who names Caesar?"

"A friend to Caesar!" Lupus said. "One who for Caesar's good would speak with Caesar!"

"Who is it?" Augustus Caesar said. "Go and look, Cornelius."

Cornelius Gallus started to go to the door, but the First Knight said, "Asinius Lupus is here."

"Oh, tell the turbulent informer to leave," Augustus Caesar said. "We have no vacant ear, now, to receive the unseasoned — unseasonable — fruits of his officious tongue."

Maecenas said to the Knights, "You must get rid of him there. Dismiss him."

The Knights forced Lupus and his companions back to the door.

"I conjure thee as thou are Caesar to respect either thine own safety or the safety of the state or both, Caesar!" Lupus said. "Hear me! Speak with me, Caesar! It is no common business I come about, but such as, being neglected, may concern the life of Caesar!"

"The life of Caesar? Let him enter," Augustus Caesar said.

He then said, "Virgil, keep thy seat."

Lupus and the Lictors approached the dais.

The Knights said to Tucca, Crispinus, Demetrius, and Aesop, "Bear back, there! Where are you going! Keep back!"

Crispinus, Demetrius, and Aesop were pushed back.

Tucca pushed past the Knights and said, "By your leave, goodman usher. Mend thy peruke; good."

A peruke is a wig, then fashionable. In pushing past the Knight, Tucca had knocked it awry. The Knight pulled it back into the right place.

"Lay hold on Horace there, and on Maecenas, Lictors!" Lupus said.

The Lictors placed them under guard. Gallus and Tibullus started forward.

Lupus said, "Romans, offer no rescue, upon your allegiance."

He gave Caesar the paper and said, "Read, royal Caesar."

He then said to Horace, "I'll tickle you, satyr!"

"He will, Humors, he will," Tucca said. "He will squeeze you, poet puckfist."

A puckfist is a puffball mushroom.

Tucca was calling Horace "Humors" as well as a mushroom — a social upstart.

Ben Jonson wrote plays about humors — personal characteristics and quirks.

Humors can also be bodily fluids. Thus Tucca's "squeeze."

Lupus said to Horace, "I'll lop you off for an unprofitable branch, you satirical varlet!"

Tucca said, "Aye, and" — he pointed to Maecenas — "Epaminondas, your patron here, with his flagon chain."

A chain is a necklace; sometimes, a small flagon of perfume hung from it.

Epaminondas was a Theban general.

Tucca then said to Maecenas, "Come, resign it. Give it up. Even if it were your great-grandfather's, the law has made it mine now, sir."

He took Maecenas' chain.

Tucca then said to the Lictors, "Look to him, my particolored rascals; look to him."

The "particolored rascals" were the Lictors, who wore multi-colored uniforms.

Pointing to the paper, Augustus Caesar said, "What is this, Asinius Lupus? I don't understand it."

"Not understand it?" Lupus said. "It is a libel, Caesar. A dangerous, seditious libel! A libel in picture."

"A libel?" Augustus Caesar said.

"Aye, I found it in this Horace's study, in Maecenas' house, here," Lupus said. "I call for the penalty of the laws against them!"

Tucca said to Lupus, "Aye, and remember to beg their land promptly, before some of these hungry, greedy court-hounds scent it out."

In Elizabethan England, a person who turned in a traitor would be rewarded with all or part of that person's land and wealth. This was called begging their land. Tucca had already claimed Maecenas' flagon chain.

Handing the paper to a Lictor, Augustus Caesar said, "Show it to Horace. Ask him if he knows it."

"Know it?" Lupus said. "His handwriting is on it, Caesar."

"Then it is no libel," Augustus Caesar said.

Augustus Caesar knew and trusted Horace enough to believe that he was not libelous or treasonous.

Horace glanced at the paper and said, "It is the imperfect — incomplete — body of an emblem, Caesar, that I began to create for Maecenas."

An emblem is a symbolic picture, often accompanied by a maxim and sometimes by explanatory verses.

"An emblem?" Lupus said. "Right. That's Greek for a libel. Do but notice how confident he is."

Horace said:

"A just man cannot fear, thou foolish Tribune.

"Not though the malice of traducing tongues, the open vastness of a tyrant's ear, the senseless rigor of the wrested laws, or the red eyes of strained authority should in a point meet all to take his life.

"His innocence is armor against all these."

"Innocence? Oh, impudence!" Lupus said.

He took back the paper and said:

"Let me see, let me see.

"Isn't here an eagle? And isn't that eagle intended to mean Caesar? Huh? Doesn't Caesar bear the eagle as insignia?"

He asked Horace, "Answer me; what do thou say?"

"Have thou any evasion, stinkard?" Tucca asked Horace.

"Now he's turned dumb," Lupus said.

He then said to Horace, "I'll tickle you, satyr."

Horace then said to express his contempt for Lupus, "Pish."

He began to laugh: "Ha! Ha!"

"Do thou pish me?" Lupus said.

He said to the Lictor carrying his sword, "Give me my long-sword."

Horace said:

"With reverence to great Caesar: worthy Romans" — he pointed to Lupus — "just observe this ridiculous commenter. The soul to my device was in this distich, aka couplet:

"'*Thus, oft [often] the base and ravenous multitude*

"'*Survive to share the spoils of fortitude,*'

"Which in this body I have figured here: A vulture —"

"A vulture?" Lupus interrupted. "Aye, now it is a vulture. Oh, abominable! Monstrous! Monstrous! Hasn't your vulture a beak? Hasn't it legs? And talons? And wings? And feathers?"

Tucca said to Lupus, "Touch him, old Buskins."

Buskins are boots.

In fencing, a touch scores a hit. The fencer touches his opponent with his weapon.

"And therefore it must be an eagle?" Horace asked.

"Don't pay him any attention, good Horace," Maecenas said. "Describe your emblem."

"A vulture and a wolf —"

"A wolf?" Lupus interrupted. "Good. That's I; I am the wolf. My name's Lupus; I am meant by the wolf. Go on, go on: a vulture and a wolf —"

Horace continued, "— preying upon the carcass of an ass —"

"An ass?" Lupus interrupted. "Good still: that's I, too. I am the ass. You mean me by the ass —"

His name was Asinius Lupus. In Latin, *asinus* means "ass," and *lupus* means "wolf."

Maecenas said to Lupus, "Please, stop braying then."

Horace said to Lupus, "If you will needs take it, I cannot with modesty give it from you."

Lupus was claiming that he was the ass, and so Horace was claiming that he could not give the title of "ass" to anyone or anything else.

Maecenas pointed out that to the Egyptians, the ass was a noble beast: "But the old Egyptians were accustomed to use the ass as a figure in their hieroglyphics to represent patience, frugality, and fortitude. We can suspect you of having none of these qualities, Tribune."

Augustus Caesar asked, "Who was it, Lupus, who informed you first that this should be meant by us? Or was it your comment — your own explanation?"

He was asking, Who told you that this figure represented us?

The figure was the eagle or vulture.

Lupus answered, "It's not my own explanation, Caesar: An actor gave me the explanation at the first sight of it, indeed."

"Aye, an honest sycophant-like slave, and a politician — a person of intrigue — besides," Tucca said.

"Where is that actor?" Augustus Caesar asked.

"He is outside, but he is here," Tucca said.

"Call him in," Augustus Caesar said.

Tucca said to the Knights, "Call in the actor there: He is Master Aesop. Call him."

The Knights called, "Actor! Where is the actor?"

Aesop the actor entered. Crispinus and Demetrius attempted to enter, but the Knights barred their way and said, "Keep back! None but the actor may enter."

Tucca pointed to Crispinus and Demetrius and said, "Yes, this gent'man and his Achates must enter."

Achates was one of Aeneas' subordinates in Virgil's *Aeneid*. Tucca was using "Achates" to refer to Demetrius.

"This gent'man," aka Crispinus, would then be Aeneas.

Crispinus said to a Knight, "Please, master usher; we'll stand close by, here."

Aesop approached the dais; Crispinus and Demetrius went inside the room.

Indicating Crispinus, Tucca said, "He is a gent'man of quality, this, although he is somewhat out of clothes, I tell ye."

He then asked the actor, "Come, Aesop; have thou a bay leaf in thy mouth?"

Aesop nodded.

The bay leaf could be aromatic and cover the smell of alcohol or bad breath, or Aesop could hold it in his mouth in the hope that it would make him eloquent. Laurel — bay — wreaths were given as an honor to exceptional people.

Tucca said, "Well done; don't be at a loss for words, stinkard. Thou shall have a monopoly of acting confirmed to thee and thy covey — thy brood — under the Emperor's broad seal, for this service."

Augustus Caesar asked Lupus about Aesop, "Is he the actor?"

"Aye, Caesar, this is he," Lupus said.

Augustus Caesar said:

"Let him be whipped.

"Lictors, take him away from here."

Some Lictors exited with Aesop.

Augustus Caesar said:

"And, Lupus, for your fierce — zealous — credulity —

"One of you outfit him with a pair of larger ears — ass' ears.

"It is Caesar's sentence, and it must not be revoked. We hate to have our court and peace disturbed with these quotidian — mundane — clamors.

"See that it is done."

"Caesar!" Lupus said.

"Gag him, so we may have his silence," Augustus Caesar said.

Lupus was gagged.

Virgil said:

"Caesar has acted like Caesar. Fair and just is his award against these brainless creatures.

"It is not the wholesome, sharp morality or modest anger of a satiric spirit that hurts or wounds the body of a state, but the sinister application of the malicious, ignorant, and base interpreter who will distort and strain the general scope and purpose of an author to his particular and private spleen, aka resentment."

Augustus Caesar said, "We know it, our dear Virgil, and esteem it a most dishonest practice in that man who will seem too witty in another's work."

Some critics will be witty at another's expense even if the other person does not deserve it. Caustic critic John Simon once wrote this about a young, beautiful actress: "Diana Rigg is built like a brick mausoleum with insufficient flying buttresses." (After a few weeks of embarrassment, Ms. Rigg began to think the quotation was funny.)

Gallus and Tibullus approached Caesar.

Augustus Caesar asked, "What do Cornelius Gallus and Tibullus want?"

While the three men quietly conferred, Tucca said to Maecenas:

"Nay, but as thou are a man — do thou hear? — a man of worship, and honorable —

"Wait, here, take thy chain again. Resume it, mad Maecenas. Reclaim it.

"What! Do thou think I meant to have kept it, bold boy? No; I did it just to frighten thee, I, to test how thou would take it.

"What! Will I turn shark — swindler — upon my friends? Or my friends' friends? I scorn it with my three souls."

Aristotle believed that human beings have a tripartite soul that consists of these three parts: 1) vegetative, 2) animal, and 3) rational.

Tucca continued saying to Maecenas:

"Come, I love bully Horace as well as thou do, I. It is an honest hieroglyphic."

In Tucca's culture, if you are called a bully, it means you are being called a jolly, fine fellow.

Tucca then said to Horace: "Give me thy wrist, Helicon."

By "wrist," he meant "hand."

Mount Helicon was sacred to the Muses.

Tucca continued, "Do thou think I'll second ever a rhinoceros — sneerer — of them all against thee? Huh?"

He pointed to Maecenas and said, "Or thy noble Hippocrene, here? I'll turn stage actor first, and be whipped, too; do thou see, bully?"

Hippocrene is the spring of the Muses on Mount Helicon.

Maecenas is like the Hippocrene in that he keeps the patronage flowing to people such as Horace, who is like Mount Helicon in that he is a giant of literature.

Augustus Caesar said to Gallus and Tiberius:

"You have your will — what you want —from Caesar; use it, Romans.

"Virgil shall be your Praetor, and ourself will here sit by, spectator of your sports, and think it no impeach of — no discredit to — royalty."

Praetors are basically second in command to Consuls, just as Executive Officers are second in command to Commanding Officers.

Gallus, Tibullus, and Maecenas conferred apart.

Augustus Caesar said to Virgil:

"Our ear is now too much profaned, grave Maro, with these distastes, to take thy sacred lines."

The "distastes" were the annoyances of Lupus and Aesop.

Virgil's name was Publius Virgilius Maro.

The sacred lines were lines of the *Aeneid*.

Augustus Caesar continued:

"Put up thy book, until both the time and we are fitted with more hallowed circumstance for the receiving of so divine a work."

He then said to Gallus, Tibullus, and Maecenas, "Proceed with your plan."

They replied, "We give thanks to great Caesar."

Gallus said:

"Tibullus, draw up the indictment, then, while Horace arrests them on the statute of calumny. Maecenas and I will take our places here.

"Lictors, assist Horace in making the arrest."

"I am the worst accuser under heaven," Horace said.

"Tut, you must do it," Gallus said. "It will be noble mirth and entertainment."

"I take no knowledge that they do malign me," Horace said.

In other words, he ignores their insults.

"Aye, but the world takes knowledge — it takes notice," Tibullus said.

"I wish the world knew how heartily I wish a fool should hate me!" Horace said.

If a fool hates someone, that is a compliment.

Crispinus and Demetrius were brought to the bar. They would be put on trial.

Seeing this, Tucca became worried and said to himself:

"By the body of Jupiter!

"What! Will they arraign my brisk poetaster and his poor journeyman, huh?

"I wish that I were abroad skeldering — conning — for a drachma, so that I would be out of this labyrinth again; I do feel myself turn stinkard already.

"But I must set the best face I have upon it now."

The best thing Tucca could do for himself now was to metaphorically throw his acquaintances under the bus.

He said out loud, "Well said, my divine, deft Horace, bring the whoreson detracting slaves to the bar, do. Make them hold up their spread golls; I'll give in evidence for thee, if thou are willing."

Golls are hands. They are held up when people take oaths. "Spread golls" are "open hands."

Tucca and Crispinus quietly spoke apart from the others.

Tucca said, "Take courage, Crispinus. I wish that thy man had a clean band — a clean collar!"

"Thy man" was Demetrius.

"What must we do, Captain?" Crispinus asked.

"Thou shall see soon," Tucca said. "Do not make division with thy legs so."

Crispinus' knees were shaking and knocking together because he was afraid. According to Tucca, the knocking sounded like a rapid passage — division — in a piece of music.

Pointing to Tucca, Augustus Caesar asked, "Who's he, Horace?"

"I know him only for a motion, Caesar," Horace answered.

A motion is literally a puppet, as in a puppet show. Figuratively, it is a human figure of fun.

Hearing them, Tucca said, "I am one of thy commanders, Caesar. I am a man of service and action. My name is Pantilius Tucca. I have served in thy wars against Mark Antony, I."

"Do you know him, Cornelius?" Augustus Caesar asked Gallus, who had been a general.

Cornelius Gallus answered, "He's one who has had the mustering or convoy — recruitment or escort — of a company now and then; I never noted him by any other employment."

"We will observe him better," Augustus Caesar said.

Having finished writing the indictment, Tibullus said, "Lictor, proclaim silence in the court."

"In the name of Caesar, silence!" the Lictor said.

"Let the parties, the accuser and the accused, present themselves," Tibullus said.

"The accuser and the accused: Present yourselves in court," the Lictor said.

"Here," Crispinus and Demetrius said.

"Read the indictment," Virgil ordered.

Tibullus ordered, "Rufus Laberius Crispinus and Demetrius Fannius, hold up your hands."

Tibullus then read out loud:

"*You are before this time jointly and severally — individually — indicted, and here immediately to be arraigned upon the statute of calumny, or Lex Remmia, aka Roman defamation law, the one by the name of Rufus Laberius Crispinus, alias Crispinus, poetaster and plagiarist; the other by the name of Demetrius Fannius, play dresser and plagiarist; that you, not having the fear of Phoebus Apollo or his shafts before your eyes, contrary to the peace of our liege lord, Augustus Caesar, his crown and dignity, and against the form of a statute in that case made and provided, have most ignorantly, foolishly, and (more like yourselves) maliciously gone about to deprave — that is, defame — and calumniate the person and writings of Quintus Horatius Flaccus here present: poet, and priest to the Muses; and to that end have mutually conspired and plotted, at sundry times as by several means and in sundry places, for the better accomplishing your base and envious purpose; taxing him falsely of self-love, arrogancy, impudence, railing, filching by translation, etc.*

"*Of all which calumnies and every one of them, in manner and form aforesaid, what do you answer?*

"*Are you guilty or not guilty?*"

Tucca said to Crispinus and Demetrius, "Say, 'Not guilty.'"

Crispinus and Demetrius pleaded, "Not guilty."

"How will you be tried?" Tibullus asked.

Tucca said to Crispinus and Demetrius, "Say, 'By the Roman gods and the noblest Romans.'"

Crispinus and Demetrius said, "By the Roman gods and the noblest Romans."

Virgil said to Crispinus and Demetrius, "Here sit Maecenas and Cornelius Gallus. Are you content to be tried by these?"

Tucca said to Crispinus and Demetrius, "Say, 'Aye, so long as the noble captain may be joined with them in commission.'"

Crispinus and Demetrius said, "Aye, so long as the noble captain may be joined with them in commission."

Virgil said to Horace, "What says the plaintiff?"

"I am content," Horace answered.

"Captain, then take your place," Virgil said.

Tucca said to Virgil:

"Alas, my worshipful Praetor, it is more of thy gent'ness than of my deserving, iwis."

Tucca's "gent'ness" means "gentleness," aka courtesy.

"Iwis" means "certainly."

Tucca continued:

"But since it has pleased the court to make choice of my wisdom and gravity —"

He said to Crispinus and Demetrius:

"— come, my calumnious varlets: Let's hear you talk for yourselves now an hour or two.

"What can you say? Make a noise. Act, act!"

Virgil said to the judges Gallus, Maecenas, and Tucca:

"Wait; turn and face Virgil and take an oath first.

"You shall swear by thunder-darting Jove, the King of gods, and by the genius of Augustus Caesar, by your own white and uncorrupted souls and the deep reverence of our Roman justice, to judge this case with truth and equity, as bound by your religion and your laws."

When taking an oath, a person would swear by the genius — guardian spirit — of the person's household. Augustus Caesar was the father of his country, and he wished to be regarded as its guardian spirit.

Rome, in fact, engaged in Emperor worship.

Virgil said to Tibullus, "Now read the evidence."

Tibullus took out two papers.

Virgil added, "But first ask each prisoner if that writing is theirs."

Tibullus gave a Lictor one paper and ordered, "Show this to Crispinus."

He then asked, "Crispinus, is it yours?"

Tucca said to Crispinus, "Say, 'Aye.'"

Crispinus hesitated.

Tucca said to him, "What, do thou stand upon it, pimp? Do not deny thine own Minerva, thy Pallas, the issue of thy brain!"

Minerva is the Roman name of Pallas Athena, who, according to mythology, was born fully grown from her father Jupiter's head. She was the goddess of wisdom.

"Yes, it is mine," Crispinus said.

The Lictor returned the paper to Tibullus.

Giving the Lictor the other paper, Tibullus ordered, "Show that to Demetrius."

He then asked, "Is it yours?"

"It is," Demetrius answered.

The Lictor returned the paper to Tibullus.

"There's a father who will not deny his own bastard, now, I warrant thee," Tucca said.

"Read the papers out loud," Virgil ordered.

The papers were poems by Crispinus and Demetrius criticizing Horace.

Tibullus began to read out loud the first paper, which was by Crispinus:

"*Ramp up, my genius! Be not retrograde [regressive],*

"*But boldly nominate [call] a spade, a spade.*

"*What! Shall thy lubrical [slippery] and glibbery [shifty] muse*

"*Live as if she were defunct [slackly], like [a] punk in stews?*"

"Ramp up" means "rear up." A ramping lion is a lion standing on its hind legs.

A punk in stews is a whore in a brothel.

Tucca said to himself, "Excellent!"

Tibullus continued to read Crispinus' poem out loud:

"*Alas! That were [would be] no modern [ordinary] consequence,*

"*To have cothurnal buskins [bootish boots] frighted [frightened] hence.*

"No! Teach thy incubus to poetize,

"And throw abroad [scatter] thy spurious snotteries [snot, aka filth]

"Upon that puffed-up [vainglorious] lump of barmy froth —"

An incubus is a male evil spirit that comes to and sleeps with women in the night.

"Barm" means the froth on fermenting malt liquor. The froth comes from yeast. "Barmy" can mean "frothing," and "froth" can mean "bubblehead."

Tucca said to himself, "Aha!"

Tibullus continued to read Crispinus' poem out loud:

"Or clumsy [numbed with cold] chilblained judgment, which with oath

"Magnificates [Magnifies] his merit, and bespawls [splatters with spit]

"The conscious time with humorous foam, and brawls

"As if his organons of sense [sensory organs] would crack

"The sinews of my patience. Break his back [Ruin him],

"O poets all and some, for now we list [wish]

"Of strenuous ven-ge-ance to clutch the fist!

"Subscri. Cris."

The last line means "I have signed. Crispinus."

Tucca said, "Aye, by the Virgin Mary, this was written like a Hercules in poetry, now!"

"Excellently well threatened!" Augustus Caesar said.

"Aye, and as strangely worded, Caesar," Virgil said.

Crispinus had used the fanciest words at his disposal.

"We observe it," Augustus Caesar said.

Virgil said to Tibullus, "Read the other poem out loud, now."

Tucca pointed to Demetrius and said, "This is a fellow of a good prodigal tongue, too; this'll do well."

Tibullus began to read out loud the second paper, which was by Demetrius:

"Our muse is in mind for the untrussing [exposing] a poet;

"I slip by his name, for most men do know it.

"A critic whom all the world bescumbers [shits]

"With satirical humors and lyrical numbers."

The poem describes a critic who shits on all the world by means of his satirical poetry.

Tucca said quietly to himself, "Are thou there, boy? Have you caught on that?"

Tibullus continued to read Demetrius' poem out loud:

"*And for the most part, himself does advance*

"*With much self-love and more arrogance.*"

"Good again," Tucca said to himself.

Tibullus continued to read Demetrius' poem out loud:

"*And, but that I would not be thought a prater,*

"*I could tell you he were a translator.*

"*I know the authors from whence he has stole,*

"*And could trace him, too, but that I understand them not full and whole.*"

Tucca said to himself, "That line has broken loose from all his fellows; chain him up shorter, do."

According to Demetrius, Horace is a plagiarist who steals from other authors who did not write in English.

Tibullus continued to read Demetrius' poem out loud:

"*The best note I can give you to know him by*

"*Is, that he keeps gallants company,*

"*Whom I would wish in time should him fear,*

"*Lest after [afterward] they buy repentance too dear [at too high a price].*

"*Subscri. Deme. Fan.*"

The last line means "I have signed. Demetrius Fannius."

"Well said," Tucca said. "This carries palm with it."

Palm leaves are signs of victory. Tucca was highly praising Demetrius' poem.

Horace said to Demetrius:

"And why, thou motley gull?"

A gull is a fool. "Motley' is multi-colored clothing worn by a jester. Demetrius' clothing consists of odds and ends of various colors.

Horace continued:

"Why should they fear? When have thou known us to wrong or tax a friend? I dare thy malice to betray it. Speak. Now thou curl up, thou poor and nasty snake, and shrink thy poisonous head into thy bosom."

Demetrius was hanging his head in shame.

Horace continued:

"Out, viper, thou that eat thy parents, hence!"

In this society, people believed that vipers were born by biting their way out of the parent's body. Vipers were symbols of ingratitude.

Horace continued:

"Rather such speckled creatures as thyself should be eschewed and shunned, such as will bite and gnaw their absent friends, not care for their friends' reputation; catch at the loosest laughters, and affect to be thought jesters; such as can devise things never seen or heard, to impair men's names and gratify their credulous adversaries; will carry tales, do basest offices, cherish divided fires, and still increase new flames out of old embers; will reveal each secret that's committed to their trust."

"Divided fires" indicate hatred between people.

Eteocles and Polynices were two brothers who agreed to take turns ruling the city of Thebes. One brother was supposed to rule for a year, and then the other brother would rule for a year, and so on. Eteocles ruled for the first year, but then he refused to give up the throne so that his brother could rule for a year. Angry, Polynices gathered an army together and marched against Thebes, creating the story of the Seven [Champions] Against Thebes. The two brothers killed each other in combat, and when their corpses were cremated together, the flame split in two over their corpses because even in death they were still angry at each other.

In Dante's *Inferno*, Ulysses and Diomedes are encased in flame together because they are angry at each other; the tip of the flame is divided in two. Both of them mourn the fall of Troy, and Diomedes is angry at Ulysses because he thought up the trick of the Trojan Horse, which finally resulted in Troy's fall.

Horace continued:

"Such men as these are black — evil — slaves; Romans, take heed of these."

Tucca said, "Thou twang — sing — right, little Horace, they are indeed: a couple of chapfallen — slack-jawed — curs."

He then said to Gallus and Maecenas, "Come, we of the bench, let's rise and go to the urn and condemn them quickly."

Jurors cast their votes — guilty or not guilty — into an urn.

As Augustus Caesar's representative, Virgil used the majestic plural as he gave instructions to the jurors Gallus, Maecenas, and Tucca:

"Before you jurors withdraw and consult together, worthy Romans, we are to tender our opinion and give you those instructions that may add to your even, impartial judgment and verdict in the case —

"Which thus we do commence. First, you must know that where there is a true and perfect merit there can be no dejection and lowering of standards, and the scorn of humble baseness often so works in a high soul upon the grosser spirit that to the grosser spirit's bleared and offended sense there seems a hideous fault blazed in the object and published to the world, when only the disease is in his eyes."

Often, a superior person's lack of false modesty appears to be a fault to a lesser person, but the fault is in the lesser person and not in the superior person.

Virgil continued:

"Because of that, it happens that our Horace now stands taxed of — charged with — impudence, self-love, and arrogance by these men, who share no merit in themselves, and therefore think his portion is as small as theirs.

"For they from their own guilt assure their souls that if they should confidently praise their works, in them it would appear inflation and self-conceit.

"But this in a full and well-digested — well-read and well-disposed and well-ordered — man cannot receive that foul abusive name of self-conceit, but instead will receive the fair title of erection — that is, advancement and elevation.

"And for his true use of translating the works of other men, it always has been a work of as much palm — success — in clearest judgments as to invent or make poetry.

"His satiric sharpness is most excusable, as being forced out of a suffering virtue oppressed with the license of the time.

"And howsoever fools or jerking — scourging — pedants, actors, or suchlike buffoonish, barking wits may with their beggarly and barren trash tickle and please base, vulgar ears with their despite and contumely,

"This maxim, like Jove's thunder, shall their pride control:

"The honest satyr — truthful satirist — has the happiest soul.

"Now, Romans, you have heard our thoughts. Withdraw when you please."

Tibullus said to the Lictors, "Remove the accused from the bar."

Tucca asked, "Who holds the urn up to us so we can vote, huh?"

He then whispered to Crispinus and Demetrius, "Fear nothing. I'll acquit you, my honest pitiful stinkards. I'll do it."

Crispinus said, "Captain, you shall eternally gird me to you, on my word as a generous, magnanimous man."

"Go to," Tucca said. "I'm blushing. Really, I am."

Maecenas, Gallus, and Tucca withdrew and consulted among themselves.

Augustus Caesar said, "Tibullus, let there be a case of vizards — a pair of masks — privately provided; we have found a subject to bestow them on."

"It shall be done, Caesar," Tibullus said.

"Here are words, Horace, able to bastinado — beat — a man's ears," Augustus Caesar said.

Horace replied, "Aye. If it pleases great Caesar, I have pills about me mixed with the whitest kind of hellebore — the best medicine of this kind — that would give him a light vomit, which should purge his brain and stomach of those tumorous heats — those swollen inflammations — if I could have permission to administer these pills to him."

"Oh, be his Aesculapius, gentle Horace!" Augustus Caesar said. "You shall have permission, and he shall be your patient."

Aesculapius was the first physician. When he died, he became the god of medicine.

Augustus Caesar then said, "Virgil, use your authority; command him to come forth."

Virgil said, "Caesar is concerned about your health, Crispinus, and he himself has chosen a physician to treat you; take his pills."

Crispinus was brought to Horace and accepted the medicine. He swallowed a pill.

Horace said, "They are somewhat bitter, sir, but very wholesome. Take yet another. Good. Stand nearby, they'll work good."

Tibullus said:

"Romans, return to your individual seats.

"Lictors, bring forward the urn, and set the accused at the bar."

The jurymen sat.

Tucca said to Crispinus and Demetrius, "Quickly, you whoreson egregious varlets! Come forward. What! Shall we sit in judgment all day upon you? You make no more haste now than a beggar upon pattens, or a physician to a patient who has no money, you pilchers."

Pattens are thick-soled shoes. Pilchers are worthless people.

Some Lictors brought the accused to the bar and brought the urn to the jurymen, who marked and placed their ballots in it. The urn was brought to Tibullus.

Tibullus said, "Rufus Laberius Crispinus and Demetrius Fannius, hold up your hands. You have, according to the Roman custom, put yourselves upon trial to the urn, for diverse and sundry calumnies whereof you have before this time been indicted and are now presently arraigned. Prepare yourselves to hearken to the verdict of your triers."

Tibullus took the ballots from the urn, looked at them and said:

"Caius Cilnius Maecenas pronounces you, by this handwriting, guilty.

"Cornelius Gallus, guilty.

"Pantilius Tucca —"

Tucca interrupted: "— parcel-guilty, I."

This means "partly guilty." Tucca was trying to have it both ways, but his vote was actually either guilty or not guilty, since those were the only verdicts allowed.

Demetrius said, "He means himself; for it was he, indeed, who suborned us to the calumny."

Tucca said to Demetrius, "I, you whoreson cantharides? Was it I?"

A cantharides is a beetle that can cause human skin to blister. Tucca was accusing Demetrius of blistering his reputation.

"I appeal to your conscience, Captain," Demetrius said to Tucca.

Tibullus said to Demetrius, "Then you confess it now."

"I do, and I crave the mercy of the court," Demetrius said.

"What does Crispinus say?" Tibullus asked.

Crispinus groaned and said, "Oh, the captain, the captain —"

"My medicine begins to work with my patient, I see," Horace said.

"Captain, stand forth and answer," Virgil said to Tucca.

Tucca replied, "Hold thy peace, poet Praetor; I appeal from thee to Caesar, I."

"Poet Praetor" resembles "poet prater."

Tucca then said to Augustus Caesar, "Do me right, royal Caesar."

Augustus Caesar replied, "By the Virgin Mary, and I will, sir."

He then ordered, "Lictors, gag him, do, and put a pair of masks over his head, so that he may look bifronted, just as he speaks."

The masks on his head would face in opposite directions — forward and backward — because Tucca was duplicitous: two-faced.

Tucca said:

"Gods and fiends! Caesar! Thou will not, Caesar, will thou?"

The Lictors approached him with a gag and two masks.

Tucca said:

"Away, you whoreson vultures, away! You think I am a dead corpse now, because Caesar is disposed to jest with a man of mark and distinction, or so."

The Lictors put their hands on him.

Tucca said:

"Hold your hooked talons out of my flesh, you inhuman harpies! Go to, do it!"

Harpies are half-bird, half-woman creatures.

Tucca continued:

"What! Will the royal Augustus cast away a gent'man of worship, a captain and a commander, for a couple of condemned caitiff calumnious cargoes?"

"Caitif" means "wretched," or "captive."

"Dispatch, Lictors," Augustus Caesar ordered. "Do it."

"Caesar!" Tucca appealed.

The Lictors gagged and masked Tucca, and then they moved him aside.

"Continue, Tibullus," Augustus Caesar said.

Virgil said to Tibullus, "Demand what cause — what reason — they had to malign Horace."

Demetrius said, "In truth, no great cause, not I, I must confess, but that he kept better company (for the most part) than I; and that better men loved him than loved me; and that his writings thrived better than mine, and were better liked, and graced; nothing else."

"Thus envious souls repine at others' good," Virgil said.

Horace said to Demetrius:

"If this is all, truly, I forgive thee freely.

"Envy me always, as long as Virgil loves me, Gallus, Tibullus, and the best-best Caesar, my dear Maecenas. While these, with many more, whose names I wisely slip, shall think me worthy their honored and adored society, and read, and love, approve, and applaud my poems, I would not wish but such as you should regard my poems with spite and contempt."

Crispinus groaned, "Oh —"

Tibullus asked, "How are thou now, Crispinus?"

He replied, "Oh, I am sick —"

Horace said, "A basin, a basin quickly! Our medicine is working."

He then said to Crispinus, "Don't faint, man. "

A receptacle was brought and held up for Crispinus.

Crispinus retched and said, "Oh — retrograde — reciprocal — incubus —"

"What's that, Horace?" Augustus Caesar asked.

Augustus Caesar was far enough away that he did not clearly hear Crispinus, and so Horace reported on the words that Crispinus was vomiting.

Horace said, "'Retrograde' and 'reciprocal incubus' have come up."

"Thanks be to Jupiter," Gallus said.

Crispinus retched and said, "Oh — glibbery — lubrical — defunct — oh! —"

"Well said; here's some abundance of inflated, pretentious words," Horace said.

"What are they?" Virgil asked.

Horace replied, "'Glibbery,' 'lubrical,' and 'defunct.'"

"Oh, they came up easy," Gallus said.

Crispinus retched and moaned, "Oh — oh! —"

"What's that?" Tibullus asked.

"Nothing yet," Horace answered.

Crispinus retched and said, "Magnificate!"

"'Magnificate'?" Maecenas said. "That came up somewhat hard."

Crispinus retched and said, "Oh, I shall cast up my — spurious — snotteries —"

Horace said to Crispinus, "Good. Again."

Crispinus retched and said, "Chilblained — oh! — oh! — clumsy —"

"That 'clumsy' stuck terribly," Horace said.

"What's all that, Horace?" Maecenas asked.

Horace answered, "'Spurious snotteries,' 'chilblained,' 'clumsy.'"

"Oh, Jupiter!" Tibullus said.

"Who would have thought there should have been such a deal of filth in a poet?" Gallus said.

Crispinus retched and said, "Oh — barmy froth —"

"What's that?" Augustus Caesar asked.

Crispinus retched and said, "Puffy — inflate — turgidous — ventositous —"

"Turgidous" means "swollen."

"Ventositous" means "flatulent" or "windy."

Horace said, "'Barmy froth,' 'puffy,' 'inflate,' 'turgidous,' and 'ventositous' have come up."

"Oh, terrible windy words!" Tibullus said.

"A sign of a windy brain," Gallus said.

Crispinus retched and said, "Oh — oblatrant — furibund — fatuate — strenuous —"

"Oblatrant" means "railing."

"Furibund" means "furious."

"Fatuate" means "speak or act foolishly."

Horace said, "Here's a deal: 'oblatrant,' 'furibund,' 'fatuate,' 'strenuous.'"

"Now all's come up, I think," Augustus Caesar said. "What a tumult he had in his belly!"

"No, not yet," Horace said. "There's the frequent 'conscious damp' behind, still."

Crispinus retched and said, "Oh — conscious — damp."

"It's come up, thanks to Apollo and Aesculapius," Horace said.

Observing Crispinus, he said, "Yet there's another; you had best take another pill."

Crispinus said, "Oh, no."

Then he moaned, "Oh! — oh! — oh! — oh!"

"Force yourself, then, a little with your finger," Horace said.

Putting his finger down his throat, Crispinus said, "Oh — oh! — prorumped!"

"Prorumped" means "burst forth."

Tibullus said, "'Prorumped'? What a noise it made! As if his spirit would have prorumped with it."

Crispinus moaned, "Oh — oh! — oh!"

"Help him," Virgil said. "It sticks strangely in his throat, whatever it is."

Crispinus retched and said, "Oh — clutched."

Horace said, "Now it's come: 'clutched.'"

"'Clutched'?" Augustus Caesar said. "It's well that's come up! It had only a narrow passage."

Crispinus retched and moaned, "Oh —"

"Again," Virgil said. "Hold him; hold his head there."

Horace supported Crispinus' head over the receptacle.

Crispinus retched and said, "Snarling gusts — quaking custard."

"Snarling gusts" can be "snarling outbursts of words."

A "quaking custard" is a "trembling coward."

"How are you now, Crispinus?" Horace asked.

Crispinus retched and said, "Oh — obstupefact!"

"Obstupefact" means "stupefied."

"We are all that, I assure you," Tibullus said.

"How do you feel?" Horace asked.

"Pretty well, I thank you," Crispinus said.

Virgil said:

"These pills can but restore him for a time, not cure him quite of such a malady, caught by so many surfeits, which have filled his blood and brain thus full of crudities.

"It is necessary, therefore, that he observe a strict and wholesome diet."

Virgil gave advice to Crispinus:

"Look that you take a good draught each morning of old Cato's principles, next your heart (that is, on an empty stomach) and then walk until it is well digested."

Some schools began teaching before breakfast, and so some learning began on an empty stomach.

Cato the Censor's style of writing was simple and straightforward, a good remedy for Crispinus' overly elaborate style.

Virgil continued giving advice to Crispinus:

"Then come home and taste a piece of Terence the comic playwright; suck his phrase instead of licorice.

"And at any hand — by all means — shun Plautus and old Ennius; they are meats too harsh for a weak stomach.

"Become accustomed to read (but not without a tutor) the best Greeks:

"These include Orpheus, Musaeus, Pindar, Hesiod, Callimachus, Theocritus, and high Homer.

"But beware of Lycophron: He is too dark and dangerous a dish."

Orpheus and Musaeus were mythical singers. Orpheus was able to make trees, stones, and floods come to him when he played. He traveled to the Land of the Dead in an attempt to rescue his wife. To get past Cerberus, the three-headed guard dog of hell, he played his lute and sang. Cerberus, put under a spell by the music, fell asleep. Orpheus was allowed to take his wife back to the Land of the Living provided that he did not look at her until she was in the Land of the Living. He led her back, stepped into the Land of the Living, and turned around to face her. Just one step away from the Land of the Living, she said to him, "Farewell," and went back down to the Land of the Dead.

Pindar was a Greek lyric poet. Theocritus was a Greek lyrical poet. Homer, of course, authored the *Iliad* and the *Odyssey*.

Lycophron used obscure words in his plays.

Virgil continued giving advice to Crispinus:

"You must not hunt for wild, outlandish terms to stuff out a peculiar — idiosyncratic — dialect, but instead let your matter — your content — run before your words.

"And if at any time you chance to meet some Gallo-Belgic phrase, you shall not immediately rack your poor verse to give it entertainment, but let it pass, and do not think yourself much damnified — damaged — if you do leave it out, when neither your understanding nor the sense could well receive it."

A semi-annual news periodical called the *Mercurius Gallobelgicus* was written in Latin.

Some phrases are not good for communicating sense.

Virgil continued giving advice to Crispinus:

"This fair abstinence in time will render you more sound and clear.

"And this I have prescribed to you, in place of a strict sentence, which until he shall perform this prescription, attire him in that robe."

Virgil pointed to it, and a Lictor dressed Crispinus in an undergraduate's gown. Crispinus would begin an education in the arts.

Virgil continued giving advice to Crispinus:

"And henceforth learn to bear yourself more humbly: not to swell, or breathe your insolent and idle spite on him whose laughter can frighten your worst attempt to slander him."

Tibullus said to the Lictors, "Take him away."

"May Jupiter guard Caesar!" Crispinus said.

Virgil said, "And for a week or two, see that he is locked up in some dark place removed from company. He will talk idly otherwise after his medicine."

People who were thought to be insane were treated by being kept alone in dark places.

Crispinus was led aside.

Virgil now said to Demetrius:

"Now to you, sir. The extremity of law awards you to be branded on the forehead for this your calumny; but since it pleases Horace, the party wronged, to entreat of Caesar a mitigation of that juster doom, with Caesar's tongue thus we pronounce your sentence.

"Demetrius Fannius, thou shall here put on" — he pointed to a fool's costume — "that coat and cap; and henceforth, think thyself no other than they make thee: a fool.

"Vow to wear them in every fair and generous assembly, until the best sort of minds shall take to knowledge as well thy satisfaction as thy wrongs."

Demetrius will wear the fool's outfit until the best minds know and acknowledge both his atonement and his offenses.

Demetrius put on the fool's clothing.

Horace said to Virgil, "Only, grave and respected Praetor, here in open court I ask that the oath for good behavior may be administered to both Crispinus and Demetrius.

"Horace, it shall," Virgil said.

He ordered, "Tibullus, give it to them."

Tibullus began to administer the oath:

"Rufus Laberius Crispinus and Demetrius Fannius, lay your hands on your hearts."

They did as asked.

Tibullus continued:

"You shall here solemnly attest and swear that never after this instant, either at booksellers' stalls, in taverns, twopenny rooms at the theater for those who pay two pennies to see a play, attiring-houses and dressing rooms, noblemen's butteries, puisnes' chambers, aka chambers for junior law students (the best and farthest places where you are admitted to come), you shall once attempt or dare (thereby to endear yourself the more to any actor, fan or friend, or guilty fool in your company) to malign, traduce, or detract the person or the writings of Quintus Horatius Flaccus or any other eminent man transcending you in merit whom your envy shall find reason to work upon, either for that or for keeping himself — the envious man — in better acquaintance or enjoying better friends."

Crispinus and Demetrius had to swear that wherever they went, they would not malign Horace or any other man better than they were, whether for the reason of tearing down the better man or for the reason of hoping to elevate themselves and to have better friends.

Tibullus continued:

"Or if — transported by any sudden and desperate resolution — you do, that then you shall not under the bastoun, or in the next presence, being an honorable assembly of his favorers, be brought as voluntary gent — a volunteer gentleman — to undertake the forswearing of it."

In other words: If you do libel a good person, then you shall not deny it because you fear a beating under the bastoun — a beating with a stick — or because you are in the presence of the man you libeled and of many of his friends who will defend him.

Tibullus continued:

"Neither shall you at any time (ambitiously affecting the title of the untrussers or whippers of the age) allow the itch of writing to overrun your performance in libel, upon pain of being taken up for lepers in wit, and — losing both your time and your papers — be irrecoverably forfeited to the Hospital of Fools."

In other words: If you succumb to the itch of libeling a better man than you are, you shall be forever sentenced to the Hospital for Fools.

Tibullus concluded:

"So help you our Roman gods and the genius of great Caesar."

Crispinus and Demetrius swore to obey the oath.

"Good," Virgil said. "Now dissolve the court."

Horace, Tibullus, Gallus, Maecenas, and Virgil all said, "And thanks to Caesar, who thus has exercised his patience."

Augustus Caesar said:

"We have indeed, you worthiest friends of Caesar.

"It is the bane and torment of our ears to hear the discords of those jangling rhymers who, with their bad and scandalous practices, bring all true arts and learning in contempt.

"But don't let your high thoughts descend so low as these despised objects: Crispinus and Demetrius. Let them decline, along with their flat, groveling souls.

"Be you yourselves.

"And as with our best favors you stand crowned, so let your mutual loves be always renowned.

"Envy will dwell where there is want [lack] of merit,

"Though the deserving man should crack his spirit."

"Crack his spirit" is like "break his heart."

All then sang this song:

"*Blush, folly, blush! Here's none who fears*

"*The wagging of an ass' ears,*

"*Although a wolfish case — exterior — he wears.*

"*Detraction is but baseness' varlet,*

"*And apes are apes, though clothed in scarlet.*"

***

Rumpatur, quisquis rumpitur invidia.

The Latin quotation, which is from Martial 9.97, means, "Let him burst, whoever is bursting with envy!"

— NOTES —

This Comical Satire was first
acted in the year
1601
By the then Children of
Queen Elizabeth's Chapel.
The principal comedians were:
NATHAN FIELD
JOHN UNDERWOOD
SALOMON PAVY
WILLIAM OSTLER
THOMAS DAY
THOMAS MARTON
With the allowance of the Master of Revels.

— 2.1 —

ALBIUS

Look here, my sweet wife: [He lays his finger on his lips.] *I am mum, my dear mummia, my balsamum, my spermaceti, and my very city of* [Aside to 55 Crispinus] *She has the most best, true, feminine wit in Rome!*
(2.1.54-56)

Source of Above:

The Cambridge Edition of the Works of Ben Jonson

7 Volume Set. Volume 2.

Ben Jonson (Author), David Bevington (Editor), Martin Butler (Editor), Ian Donaldson (Editor).

Cambridge University Press, 2012. Print. P. 50.

Here is an interesting excerpt from an article on mummia, which is part of a corpse used in preparing medicine:

The last line of a 17th century poem by John Donne prompted Louise Noble's quest. "Women," the line read, are not only "Sweetness and wit," but "mummy, possessed."

Sweetness and wit, sure. But mummy? In her search for an explanation, Noble, a lecturer of English at the University of New England in Australia, made a surprising discovery: That word recurs throughout the literature of early modern Europe, from Donne's "Love's Alchemy" to Shakespeare's "Othello" and Edmund Spenser's "The Faerie Queene," because mummies and other preserved and fresh human remains were a common ingredient in the medicine of that time. In short: Not long ago, Europeans were cannibals.

Source of Above:

Dolan, Maria: "The Gruesome History of Eating Corpses as Medicine: The question was not 'Should you eat human flesh?' says one historian, but, 'What sort of flesh should you eat?'" *The Smithsonian Magazine.* 6 May 2012 https://www.smithsonianmag.com/history/the-gruesome-history-of-eating-corpses-as-medicine-82360284/

— 5.3 —

CAESAR

> *We know it, our dear Virgil, and esteem it 125*
> *A most dishonest practice in that man*
> *Will seem too witty in another's work.*

(5.3.125-127)

Source of Above:

The Cambridge Edition of the Works of Ben Jonson

7 Volume Set. Volume 2.

Ben Jonson (Author), David Bevington (Editor), Martin Butler (Editor), Ian Donaldson (Editor).

Cambridge University Press, 2012. Print. P. 147.

The following anecdote appears in David Bruce's book *The Funniest People in Theater: 250 Anecdotes*:

After seeing actress Diana Rigg in a brief nude scene in the play *Abelard and Heloise*, caustic critic John Simon wrote, "Diana Rigg is built like a brick mausoleum with insufficient flying buttresses." The next day, as Ms. Rigg went to the theater, she hoped that no one would recognize her. Fortunately, all of the cast members knew better than to mention the review. After a few weeks, however, she began to think the review funny and soon started quoting it. (By the way, Ms. Rigg knows an actress — not herself — who saw Mr. Simon in a New York restaurant and took the opportunity to dump a plate of potato salad on his head.)

Source: Source: Diana Rigg, compiler, *No Turn Unstoned*, pp. 8, 42, 114.

The anecdote was retold in David Bruce's own words from Ms. Rigg's book: Rigg, Diana, compiler. *No Turn Unstoned: The Worst Ever Theatrical Reviews*. Los Angeles, CA: Silman-James Press, 1982.

— 5.3 —

And if at any time you chance to meet
Some Gallo-Belgic phrase, you shall not immediately 490
Rack your poor verse to give it entertainment,
But let it pass, and do not think yourself
Much damnified if you do leave it out,
When neither your understanding nor the sense
Could well receive it.

(5.3.489-495)

Source of Above:

The Cambridge Edition of the Works of Ben Jonson

7 Volume Set. Volume 2.

Ben Jonson (Author), David Bevington (Editor), Martin Butler (Editor), Ian Donaldson (Editor).

Cambridge University Press, 2012. Print. P. 164.

This is one of John Donne's Epigrams:

MERCURIUS GALLO-BELGICUS.

Like Esop's fellow-slaves, O Mercury,
Which could do all things, thy faith is ; and I
Like Esop's self, which nothing. I confess
I should have had more faith, if thou hadst less.
Thy credit lost thy credit. 'Tis sin to do,
In this case, as thou wouldst be done unto,
To believe all. Change thy name ; thou art like
Mercury in stealing, but liest like a Greek.

Source: Donne, John. "Epigrams." Poems of John Donne. Vol II. E. K. Chambers, Editor. London: Lawrence & Bullen, 1896.

http://www.luminarium.org/editions/donneepigrams.htm

This is one of Bren Jonson's Epigrams:

Source text:

XCII.

The New Cry.

Ere Cherries ripe, and Straw-berries be gon,
Unto the Crys of London I'll add one;
Ripe Statesmen, ripe: They grow in every Street;
At six and twenty, ripe. You shall 'em meet,
And have 'em yield no favour, but of State.
Ripe are their Ruffs, their Cuffs, their Beards, their Gate,
And Grave as ripe, like mellow as their Faces.
They know the States of Christendom, not the Places:
Yet have they seen the Maps, and bought 'em too,
And understand 'em, as most Chapmen do.
The Counsels, Projects, Practices they know,
And what each Prince doth for Intelligence owe,
And unto whom: They are the Almanacks
For Twelve Years yet to come, what each State lacks.
They carry in their Pockets Tacitus,
And the Gazetti, or Gallo-Belgicus:
And talk reserv'd, lock'd up, and full of fear,
Nay, ask you, how the Day goes in your Ear:
Keep a Star-Chamber Sentence close, Twelve Days:
And whisper what a Proclamation says.
They meet in Sixes, and at every Mart,
Are sure to con' the Catalogue by heart;
Or, every Day, some one at Rimee's looks,
Or Bills, and there he buys the Names of Books.
They all get Porta, for the sundry ways
To write in Cypher, and the several Keys,
To ope' the Character. They've found the slight
With Juice of Limons, Onions, Piss, to write;
To break up Seals, and close 'em. And they know,
If the States make Peace, how it will go
With England. All forbidden Books they get.
And of the Powder-Plot, they will talk yet.
At naming the French King, their Heads they shake,

179

And at the Pope, and Spain slight Faces make.
Or 'gainst the Bishops, for the Brethren, rail,
Much like those Brethren; thinking to prevail
With ignorance on us, as they have done
On them: And therefore do not only shun
Others more modest, but contemn us too,
That know not so much State, wrong, as they do.

Source of Above: *Epigrams*. Book. The Holloway Pages.
https://hollowaypages.com/jonson1692epigrams.htm

APPENDIX A: ABOUT THE AUTHOR

It was a dark and stormy night. Suddenly a cry rang out, and on a hot summer night in 1954, Josephine, wife of Carl Bruce, gave birth to a boy — me. Unfortunately, this young married couple allowed Reuben Saturday, Josephine's brother, to name their first-born. Reuben, aka "The Joker," decided that Bruce was a nice name, so he decided to name me Bruce Bruce. I have gone by my middle name — David — ever since.

Being named Bruce David Bruce hasn't been all bad. Bank tellers remember me very quickly, so I don't often have to show an ID. It can be fun in charades, also. When I was a counselor as a teenager at Camp Echoing Hills in Warsaw, Ohio, a fellow counselor gave the signs for "sounds like" and "two words," then she pointed to a bruise on her leg twice. Bruise Bruise? Oh yeah, Bruce Bruce is the answer!

Uncle Reuben, by the way, gave me a haircut when I was in kindergarten. He cut my hair short and shaved a small bald spot on the back of my head. My mother wouldn't let me go to school until the bald spot grew out again.

Of all my brothers and sisters (six in all), I am the only transplant to Athens, Ohio. I was born in Newark, Ohio, and have lived all around Southeastern Ohio. However, I moved to Athens to go to Ohio University and have never left.

At Ohio U, I never could make up my mind whether to major in English or Philosophy, so I got a bachelor's degree with a double major in both areas, then I added a Master of Arts degree in English and a Master of Arts degree in Philosophy. Yes, I have my MAMA degree.

Currently, and for a long time to come (I eat fruits and veggies), I am spending my retirement writing books such as *Nadia Comaneci: Perfect 10*, *The Funniest People in Comedy*, *Homer's* Iliad: *A Retelling in Prose*, and *William Shakespeare's* Hamlet: *A Retelling in Prose*.

By the way, my sister Brenda Kennedy writes romances such as *A New Beginning* and *Shattered Dreams*.

APPENDIX B: SOME BOOKS BY DAVID BRUCE

Retellings of a Classic Work of Literature

Arden of Faversham: *A Retelling*

Ben Jonson's The Alchemist: *A Retelling*

Ben Jonson's The Arraignment, or Poetaster: *A Retelling*

Ben Jonson's Bartholomew Fair: *A Retelling*

Ben Jonson's The Case is Altered: *A Retelling*

Ben Jonson's Catiline's Conspiracy: *A Retelling*

Ben Jonson's The Devil is an Ass: *A Retelling*

Ben Jonson's Epicene: *A Retelling*

Ben Jonson's Every Man in His Humor: *A Retelling*

Ben Jonson's Every Man Out of His Humor: *A Retelling*

Ben Jonson's The Fountain of Self-Love, or Cynthia's Revels: *A Retelling*

Ben Jonson's The Magnetic Lady, or Humors Reconciled: *A Retelling*

Ben Jonson's The New Inn, or The Light Heart: *A Retelling*

Ben Jonson's Sejanus' Fall: *A Retelling*

Ben Jonson's The Staple of News: *A Retelling*

Ben Jonson's A Tale of a Tub: *A Retelling*

Ben Jonson's Volpone, or the Fox: *A Retelling*

Christopher Marlowe's Complete Plays: Retellings

Christopher Marlowe's Dido, Queen of Carthage: *A Retelling*

Christopher Marlowe's Doctor Faustus: *Retellings of the 1604 A-Text and of the 1616 B-Text*

Christopher Marlowe's Edward II: *A Retelling*

Christopher Marlowe's The Massacre at Paris: *A Retelling*

Christopher Marlowe's The Rich Jew of Malta: *A Retelling*

Christopher Marlowe's Tamburlaine, Parts 1 and 2: *Retellings*

Dante's Divine Comedy: *A Retelling in Prose*

Dante's Inferno: *A Retelling in Prose*

Dante's Purgatory: *A Retelling in Prose*

Dante's Paradise: *A Retelling in Prose*

The Famous Victories of Henry V: *A Retelling*

From the Iliad *to the* Odyssey: *A Retelling in Prose of Quintus of Smyrna's* Posthomerica

George Chapman, Ben Jonson, and John Marston's Eastward Ho! *A Retelling*

George Peele's The Arraignment of Paris: *A Retelling*

George Peele's The Battle of Alcazar: *A Retelling*

George's Peele's David and Bathsheba, and the Tragedy of Absalom: *A Retelling*

George Peele's Edward I: *A Retelling*

George Peele's The Old Wives' Tale: *A Retelling*

William Shakespeare's 38 Plays: Retellings in Prose
William Shakespeare's 1 Henry IV, aka Henry IV, Part 1: A Retelling in Prose
William Shakespeare's 2 Henry IV, aka Henry IV, Part 2: A Retelling in Prose
William Shakespeare's 1 Henry VI, aka Henry VI, Part 1: A Retelling in Prose
William Shakespeare's 2 Henry VI, aka Henry VI, Part 2: A Retelling in Prose
William Shakespeare's 3 Henry VI, aka Henry VI, Part 3: A Retelling in Prose
William Shakespeare's All's Well that Ends Well: A Retelling in Prose
William Shakespeare's Antony and Cleopatra: A Retelling in Prose
William Shakespeare's As You Like It: A Retelling in Prose
William Shakespeare's The Comedy of Errors: A Retelling in Prose
William Shakespeare's Coriolanus: A Retelling in Prose
William Shakespeare's Cymbeline: A Retelling in Prose
William Shakespeare's Hamlet: A Retelling in Prose
William Shakespeare's Henry V: A Retelling in Prose
William Shakespeare's Henry VIII: A Retelling in Prose
William Shakespeare's Julius Caesar: A Retelling in Prose
William Shakespeare's King John: A Retelling in Prose
William Shakespeare's King Lear: A Retelling in Prose
William Shakespeare's Love's Labor's Lost: A Retelling in Prose
William Shakespeare's Macbeth: A Retelling in Prose
William Shakespeare's Measure for Measure: A Retelling in Prose
William Shakespeare's The Merchant of Venice: A Retelling in Prose
William Shakespeare's The Merry Wives of Windsor: A Retelling in Prose
William Shakespeare's A Midsummer Night's Dream: A Retelling in Prose
William Shakespeare's Much Ado About Nothing: A Retelling in Prose
William Shakespeare's Othello: A Retelling in Prose
William Shakespeare's Pericles, Prince of Tyre: A Retelling in Prose
William Shakespeare's Richard II: A Retelling in Prose
William Shakespeare's Richard III: A Retelling in Prose
William Shakespeare's Romeo and Juliet: A Retelling in Prose
William Shakespeare's The Taming of the Shrew: A Retelling in Prose
William Shakespeare's The Tempest: A Retelling in Prose
William Shakespeare's Timon of Athens: A Retelling in Prose
William Shakespeare's Titus Andronicus: A Retelling in Prose
William Shakespeare's Troilus and Cressida: A Retelling in Prose
William Shakespeare's Twelfth Night: A Retelling in Prose
William Shakespeare's The Two Gentlemen of Verona: A Retelling in Prose
William Shakespeare's The Two Noble Kinsmen: A Retelling in Prose
William Shakespeare's The Winter's Tale: A Retelling in Prose